A Fire In Her Bones

A Feral Spark, Volume 2

JD Cadmon

Published by JD Cadmon, 2023.

This is a work of fiction. Similarities to real people, places, or events are entirely coincidental.

A FIRE IN HER BONES

First edition. December 12, 2023.

Copyright © 2023 JD Cadmon.

ISBN: 979-8223064558

Written by JD Cadmon.

Also by JD Cadmon

A Feral Spark
A Feral Spark
A Fire In Her Bones

Belli & the Beat
Let's Bake A Deal

Watch for more at https://jdcadmon.carrd.co/.

Table of Contents

CHAPTER ONE

Miranda shook more than a sleigh bell at an elementary school holiday concert as she walked through the airport. The prospect of seeing her family for Christmas drew nearer with each step. Her boyfriend, Jason, took her hand and modeled calm and regular breathing, like Lamaze but without the noise.

Fitting, really.

He was literally the father of her unborn children thanks to thirteen embryos that were made against their will. Not that Miranda planned to share that particular tidbit with her family. Her return home was a mission of reconciliation, if that was even the right word. Confrontation, more likely.

In her nineteen years, this was the first time Miranda had set foot inside the small airport near her northwest Montana hometown. The first flight she had ever taken was the one out of Ithaca, New York, that morning. Months ago, she'd driven herself there to take one of the spots in Cornell University's farrier certificate program.

In New York, Miranda met Jason, a werewolf who had deduced her unique ability to manifest and control fire. They'd developed a deep bond of friendship in the four months they'd known each other that had morphed into love when neither of them was looking.

Miranda's truck was still in Ithaca, an inconvenience to her mobility in Montana. She wasn't old enough to rent a vehicle, and Jason, at twenty-four, still hadn't learned how to drive. If she believed in signs, she might think her mission to put everything right with her family was off to a less than auspicious start.

They didn't have to pick up any checked baggage, so they headed to the drop-off and loading zone. Miranda blinked against the light of the winter sun and scanned for any vehicles that might be there to fetch them. When she saw her mother's dark blue, late model sedan, Miranda flagged her down and stepped to the curb with Jason.

Christina Lennox piloted her car in front of them and parked with the hazard lights flashing. Both front doors opened, and Miranda's sister-in-law Jessica got out of the passenger side. The two women had a matching suburban wife look. Christina had a short blonde bob with blue eyes, and Jessica had dark brown hair that was short on the sides and long on top.

Miranda, on the other hand, looked like the Lennox side of the family. Her paternal grandparents had emigrated from Scotland some sixty years ago. Like the others, she had pale skin, brown eyes, and vibrant red hair that she usually wore long and in a braid. It was the most practical thing when she worked with horses. In short, Miranda could be the poster girl for all things Scottish that had escaped to the Rocky Mountains.

"How've you been, Randy?" Jessica asked with a teasing smirk.

She squinted at the other woman and let her breath out slowly. Miranda hated that nickname.

Already moving on to Jason, Jessica asked, "Who are *you*?"

The tone her sister-in-law used sounded like she thought he was the gunk normally found on the bottom of her shoe. Jason shot Miranda a questioning glance, and she possessively slid her arm around his waist.

"This is my boyfriend, Jason."

He stood six feet tall with the bushy blond hair of a guy straight out of an '80s metal band. The violin he carried added to the wild musician vibe, as did his strikingly odd silver eyes that had once been blue. Underneath his clothes, Jason had three tattoos from the genetics lab that had remade him into a werewolf. For his safety, he usually kept those hidden from view.

"You didn't tell us you were bringing anyone home," Christina said.

"I did tell you, Mom." It was like the woman enjoyed not listening to her.

"It was my fault," Jason apologized. "I wasn't sure my travel papers would be ready in time."

Miranda had been wrapped up in her own issues and hadn't fully considered his challenges. His legal identity as Jason was only five days old, but he had still agreed to come home with her. He also had to deal with the added complication of a full moon the next night. It was the same night the family and many people in the community would be celebrating her grandfather's eightieth birthday.

She offered him a secret smile as she snuggled closer to his side. Then she told her mother, "Well, we're both here. So could you try to make Jason feel welcome?"

The car behind them honked, so Christina opened the trunk and said, "Let's get moving then. We've got a lot of stuff to do."

After stowing their carry-on bags in the trunk, everyone got in the car. Miranda took the spot behind Jessica, and Jason sat behind her mother, placing his violin on the seat beside him.

From the front seat, Jessica rattled off the itinerary for the week, ticking each point off with her fingers. "Tonight we have to finish getting ready for Pops's birthday party tomorrow. Christmas

Eve with Christina and Michael is Monday. Tuesday, we go to Pops and Nan's for Christmas Day."

"Sounds like a very busy week," Jason said.

"That's right. So, if you came here to sleep and do nothing, you'll be disappointed," Jessica said as they buckled their seatbelts.

[I'm sorry she's like this,] Miranda signed. [My brother Monty loves her. I have no idea why.]

Jason tapped the top of the violin case, letting a few beats pass. [I'll be fine. I recognize her type from a few customers at the practice.]

That was what Miranda thought he signed, anyway. Her skill with Sign Language wasn't as advanced as his yet. Like many hearing children, she had dabbled with Sign when she was younger. Meeting Jason made her want to take learning ASL seriously. She improved with every conversation.

"What are you two doing back there?" Christina asked, quickly looking over her shoulder.

"Sign Language," Miranda said.

"It's my first language," Jason told her.

"I didn't realize you were deaf!" Jessica bellowed. "You don't look deaf."

"What does deaf look like?" Miranda asked with distaste.

"I can hear you just fine," Jason said with exaggerated patience. "Sign is a full language with its own rules and grammar. Sometimes I slip into it without thinking."

Snapping and pointing at him, Miranda said, "You're code switching!"

She felt pretty proud of that knowledge. Jason often used Sign Language, particularly when they were discussing sensitive topics.

"Do you have a job?" Christina asked him, using the mirror to make eye contact.

"I'm a veterinarian's assistant." Angling toward Miranda, he said, "Dr. Burgess was talking about helping me become a vet tech after I get my high school diploma. A generous offer, but I still want to become a luthier."

"Oh, that's awesome." Miranda squeezed his hand and gave him a toothy grin.

"What's a luthier?" Jessica asked.

"A stringed-instrument maker." Jason's expression became soft and dreamy. "I want to make violins."

Jessica, of course, didn't see his look and trampled all over his ambition. "Why would you want to do that? Aren't the best ones already made, like Stradivarius and such?"

"Rude!" Miranda slapped the back of Jessica's headrest.

"Stop that, Miranda." Christina directed her attention back to Jason. "What do you mean, when you get your diploma? Haven't you finished high school yet?"

"Unfortunately, no." Normal teenaged milestones didn't apply to Jason. He had been kidnapped by the genetics lab as a homeless fourteen-year-old and fully transformed into a werewolf by the time he was seventeen. "After we go back to New York, I'll look into testing for it. I need to get a driver's license too."

"No driver's license?" Christina lightly tapped on the steering wheel. "Miranda, what are *your* job prospects? Do you have something lined up?"

"Not yet. I'll start hunting again in January when we go back to New York. Jason's family has been really nice to let me stay with them while I search for a job."

She stroked the *shin* necklace that Joel Rosen, Jason's adoptive father, had given her during Hanukkah. It wasn't a typical holiday gift, but he'd done it as a representation of her internal flame. The Rosen family had given Jason safety and love when he needed it. They extended their hospitality and protection to Miranda after they'd escaped from the clutches of John Coleman.

The Rosen family had accepted Miranda, even with her unusual fire power, faster than her own family had ever done. Joel, Lurlene, and the boys helped her realize she deserved better out of life than scorn and mistreatment. They gave her the courage to come home and face her wounds.

"Well, that doesn't make sense," Jessica declared. "Shouldn't you make sure you have a job before you go traipsing all over the country?"

"When you're the one paying my bills," Miranda hissed, "then your opinion might matter to me."

"Well, you can't blame me for asking! First, you weren't coming home, but now you're here with this los—" Jessica paused her tirade and glanced back at Jason. "With this random guy for a boyfriend. I'm not the one giving mixed signals, Miranda."

Staring at the ends of Jessica's hair, Miranda fantasized about setting them on fire. She opened up her fingers as if to do it, but Jason subtly shook his head. She glowered but didn't give in to her destructive urge. The Montana countryside out the window suddenly became interesting, as if it wasn't something that she'd seen almost every day of her nineteen years.

Miranda could control combustion energy to create and extinguish fires at will. Jason called her an energy shifter, a play on words since he as a werewolf was a *shape* shifter. It was a great concept, but Miranda had never met another person who could manipulate energy.

She'd felt very lonely growing up and had shied away from most people in fear that she'd accidentally harm them. Conversely, the fire inside her made her seek out the wild in nature, such as mustangs and coyotes. Or werewolves.

Jason's warm fingers entwined with hers as Christina drove them to the grocery store. They were going to pick up party supplies before stopping at her parents' house, where they would be staying. The birthday party preparation was at Jessica's house that night, and her sister-in-law looked pleased to play hostess.

Jessica unbuckled her seatbelt. "I'll start on the list, Chrissie."

Jason turned his head to Miranda, a twinkle of mischief in his eyes. "Could we do some campfire food? Marshmallows and sausages. That would be so fun."

When she'd been practicing her fire control in New York, they often ended sessions by snacking on toasted marshmallows. "Yeah, sure. Sounds like fun."

The four of them got out of the car, and Jason paused on the threshold before entering the store.

[Too many sounds and smells,] he explained in Sign.

"Take your time," Miranda said with a gentle touch to his back.

She'd seen it before when Jason had to enter places that had a lot of people, such as shopping malls or even the concert hall where the community orchestra had played *Messiah*. Then again, those could have been nerves of a different sort.

After fortifying his internal defenses, Jason strode into the store. Miranda told her mother that she had to use the bathroom.

"I'll go with you." Christina said, coming back to her.

Miranda tried and failed to stop herself from rolling her eyes. Without Jason or even Jessica as a social buffer, Christina's bitchy side would come out.

After a quick visual check that no one else was in the bathroom, Christina demanded, "Why did you really come home? And why did you bring that man?"

"He's my boyfriend. I love him. I want him to meet my family for the holidays," she said sweetly. "And Pops's eightieth birthday is tomorrow. I don't want to miss that."

Christina threw her head back and laughed. "What's the real reason?"

She wasn't sure of the diplomatic way to say it, so Miranda chose the most scandalous option. "I'm here to set the world on fire."

Her mother gasped and put her palm out as if to clamp it over Miranda's mouth. "You can't say that! What would your boyfriend think if he knew about the real you? The one who destroys everything?"

"Considering he already knows who I am, he'll probably roast his marshmallows and watch the world burn with me."

Just as there was an art to making an entrance, Miranda hoped her words were sharp enough to be the soundtrack of her exit.

CHAPTER TWO

The house where Miranda had spent most of her childhood was far outside the city limits, nestled in a protected meadow of mountain foothills and tall pine trees. It was a picturesque setting out of an Alpine dream. A wrap-around porch that had been a summer gathering place encircled the two-story home. In addition to the main house, there was a separate multi-car garage and a barn for equipment and her parents' horses.

Miranda's parents had moved into the house after her childhood "church incident," as some called it. Her brothers had not enjoyed having to change schools halfway through high school. At least Monty, the oldest of her brothers, had gone to the University of Montana on early admission and had already been on campus.

As they pulled up to the property, Jason nudged her and asked, "Do I get to meet your horse?"

Miranda didn't have a horse of her own. Her favorite had been Pops's horse Betsy, and after the mare died when Miranda was thirteen, she hadn't gotten a horse for herself. She kept busy by caring for her parents' horses and taking a job as a groom and trail ride guide for visiting tourists.

"I'll introduce you to the horses later, but none of them are mine. It would have been harder to take a job offer in New York if I had a horse waiting for me."

In addition to her farrier course at Cornell, Miranda had worked in a private stable teaching a rich man's son western riding.

She'd met Jason at a frat party, though she wouldn't have guessed upon first seeing him that he was a werewolf. He had her number, though, asking about her light-filled aura.

"Hey," Jason whispered. [Everything okay?]

She wasn't sure. Miranda honestly had no clue how to connect with her family. It was worse than meeting actual strangers who had no preconceived notions about who you were. Family had plenty of notions and limited flexibility to change their minds when presented with the truth.

Christina interrupted her thoughts. "Help bring the groceries in."

"Right," Miranda said with a nod. Then she pointed at her father's truck in the garage. "Dad's going to help with the party too, right?"

"Sort of," her mother replied. "He and your Uncle Ronald are going to keep Pops occupied and out of the way while the rest of us finish assembling party favors."

In a needlessly loud voice meant to include Jason, Jessica asked, "Are you okay with that after traveling all day?"

He shrugged. "Whatever Miranda wants is fine with me."

"Of course, we'll help," she told Jessica, "after we put our luggage away in my room."

Christina pressed her lips together. "You don't think he's sleeping with you, do you? We have other rooms in this house he can take."

"You don't need to get another room ready," Miranda said. She had to bite her tongue not to add that her mom had forgotten he was coming in the first place.

Though she and Jason stayed in separate rooms at the Rosen house, here she wanted his supportive presence beside her.

Unfortunately, they'd have to sleep on the floor, because her twin bed wouldn't be big enough for the both of them without extreme spooning.

"I guess that means you're special," Jessica told Jason at a normal volume. "Miranda's never brought one of her boys home before."

"But she definitely dated a lot," Christina said flatly.

There had never been a reason to bring those disposable boys home. Miranda had an active sex life with no emotional attachments during high school and the year before she went to New York. As she didn't otherwise like people too much, the sex hadn't been all that fulfilling.

Jason affected wide-eyed innocence as he said, "I, too, never brought a boy home, but I definitely dated a lot."

Miranda snorted at his sass. Jason had never used a convenient label for his sexual orientation other than telling her he wasn't straight. As long as he wanted to be with her, she wasn't bothered by his queerness.

Firm in her decision, Miranda said, "We're going to stay in my room together."

"I don't like it." Christina's eyes darted back and forth between them. "Make sure you use condoms if you must."

Blinking in surprise, Miranda shook her head. *Of course* they used condoms when they had sex. Not that they were doing it at every available opportunity. Both she and Jason had intimacy issues they were still unpacking.

"We'll be responsible, Mom."

Christina's pinched lips were a sign she still wasn't happy about it, but she led them into the house through a side door, into a kitchen with a big farmhouse sink and maple brown cabinets. They all took several trips back and forth to the car to get the bags of groceries, making unloading a quick and painless job.

"I'll help put everything away," Jessica said, "if you two take out the trash."

"Thanks!" Miranda hadn't expected the other woman's kindness when it came to the division of labor.

After they retrieved their luggage from the entrance, Miranda guided Jason into the big living room with a vaulted ceiling and a fireplace. The year-round decorating touches had cowboy elements with some Scottish flair for accent, such as the Lennox clan tartan and symbolic weapons above the mantel.

In acknowledgment of the Christmas season, an artificial tree decorated with strings of lights, tinsel garlands, and various ornaments stood tall under the highest part of the ceiling. Underneath the tree was a toy store's worth of presents for Miranda's nieces and nephews. Christmas stockings with all the children's names hung by the fireplace. Holiday pine-scented wax in warming dishes added to the ambience. Miranda liked the smell, but Jason didn't, if the way he rubbed his nose was anything to go by.

"At least it's not peppermint," he said. "I'd have to sleep in the barn."

Jason absolutely hated peppermint thanks to John Coleman, who had been one of the geneticists working on the werewolf project. Before Coleman kidnapped them at Thanksgiving, Miranda had been indifferent. Now she hated it just as much as Jason did.

"I'd have to join you if it was peppermint. Come on, I'll show you my room."

Upstairs, Miranda's bedroom was right beside her parents' master suite. As the youngest child with a significant age gap from her nearest sibling, it was one of the ways they'd monitored her. Yet another reason why high school Miranda never brought a boy home.

Miranda paused at the door and let out a long breath. She didn't have time to get philosophical about who she was now compared to who she had been before her time in New York. Being in her old room again might force her to look closely at herself, and she hoped she'd still like what she saw.

Turning the round knob that wasn't very werewolf-friendly, Miranda stepped through to a room that was decorated in pink camouflage and horse trappings. She had photos of her trail rides on a bulletin board, 4-H certificates and trophies, some of the tassels from her high school graduation, and a stack of information about the farrier programs at places other than Cornell. While recognizably hers, it felt like something that belonged to a person she'd left behind.

"Twin bed," Jason said behind her. "So I'm in a sleeping bag or in wolf skin?"

"I wouldn't recommend it." Miranda pointed to the door handle that he wouldn't easily open without thumbs. "I'll join you on the floor. We'll put pillows and blankets down like we do on the air mattress at home."

The ease with which the word slipped out of her mouth startled her. This was the home Miranda had lived in since she was six years old. Yet in a ridiculously short time, the Rosen house in Ithaca had become what truly felt like home.

Miranda set her suitcase by the closet near her bedroom door and opened it up to look at her clothes. Her normal outfits consisted of jeans, t-shirts, flannel shirts, and the occasional snapback hat. Inside the closet, she also had a folk-style dress from Scotland in a specific blue and white plaid.

Jason ran his index finger over the skirt fabric. "I sense a theme."

"My clan tartan. I'll wear it to Pops's birthday party tomorrow."

"I'm sure you'll look beautiful." Jason pecked her cheek. "You already do."

Miranda turned into him to feel the strength of his body against hers. Jason was a person she was in the process of learning, and she had no delusions that she knew all there was to know about him. His character, though, resonated with hers. When she was with him, her spirit felt at rest. Precious little else in her life gave her that sense of calm.

"So, Pops," Jason started delicately after releasing the hug, "he doesn't play anymore because you burned his hand when he rescued you?"

Her grandfather had been a fiddler with an impressive reputation all over the region until Miranda accidentally mangled his hand. She wore the guilt like a shadow over her soul. Her stories about Pops had been a touchstone for both of them. Jason, as a former violin prodigy who'd only recently returned to music, had told her of his deep sympathy for the other man.

"Yeah, I did that," she confirmed. "That was almost fourteen years ago."

Jason winced as he set his violin on a secure shelf. He turned to Miranda with his hands raised as if to use Sign Language. "I've been wondering something about that. How did he know where to find you?"

Miranda frowned as disjointed images of the night played on the screen of her memory. As a five-year-old, the adults hadn't told her much about what they knew. Pops had been there, though, and his hands had been the last that had touched her before she got free.

[I don't know,] she signed slowly. She should know, shouldn't she? It was her own life and a rather formative event.

Shattering the ponderous calm, her father shouted, "Miranda Claire!"

Michael Lennox stood in her doorway, all stocky figure and auburn hair. Their genetic similarity was strong, but that didn't explain why she was the only one in her family who could manipulate fire.

"Hi, Dad," she said with an awkward wave.

Her father's gaze swept from the top of her head to her sock-clad feet and back to her face. "Good of you to make it home for your grandfather's big birthday."

"It was the right thing to do."

"Your brother Mason won't be here," Michael said gruffly. "Went south to spend the holidays with his in-laws. Avoiding bad weather if you ask me."

Her father's assessing look moved on to Jason, the strange man standing in his daughter's childhood bedroom. Miranda preemptively sighed because she expected macho posturing.

"This is my boyfriend, Jason Rosen."

The two men shook hands, Michael squeezing so tightly his own veins popped. "I know nothing about you. Don't come into my house thinking you can disrespect me by doing anything you want to my daughter."

"Dad!"

He ignored her and kept gripping Jason's hand. "Where are you from? How'd you two meet?"

"Chicago, originally. At a frat party," Jason answered and extracted his hand.

"Do you have any ambition, or are you a lazy bum?"

Jason shot him an incredulous look before signing to Miranda. [Will we have to do this with everyone we meet?]

It wasn't actually funny, but she couldn't hold back a laugh. "We could make baseball cards with our relationship stats on them."

Michael looked unamused and flicked his fingers in Jason's direction. "I don't care what this is with the hands. Answer the question."

"Sure." Jason stood in a pose similar to parade rest with his hands behind his back. "I've got a job with a good boss. I'm looking at options for how to get my dream job. I'm still getting used to having a choice."

"That will have to do for now. I have to go, but I'll be watching you." Michael nodded first to Jason and then to Miranda. "Ronald and I have to distract our father while the rest of you finish prepping the last of his party. He'll probably tell us about the glory of Scotland and what disappointments we are."

As he descended the stairs, Miranda shouted, "Love you, Dad."

He put his hand in the air and swatted the invisible words away like they weren't necessary.

After he was gone, Jason asked, "Did I pass?"

"Most of the time, I don't know if *I* pass." Miranda shrugged. "We can fail together."

Jason put his hand over his heart and stepped back with a pinched look on his face.

[What's wrong?] Miranda signed.

[The full moon. This is going to be a strong one.]

It would hit him tomorrow in the early evening, around 6:00 p.m., and he'd be locked into his wolf shape for thirteen hours. Even knowing that, he'd still agreed to come with her to Montana because she wanted him there.

"You're a really good boyfriend."

Miranda offered up a kiss that he thoroughly reciprocated, his hands on her lower back, pulling her body into his. As her hands glided over his supple spine, Miranda marveled how Jason felt like home. It was so entirely sappy, a vulnerable and happy emotion she had never felt before. Others would say it was merely the intoxication of a new relationship. That was possible but not the whole of it. Jason saw her as she truly was and was unafraid.

When they ended their kiss, Miranda leaned her forehead against his shoulder.

"I guess we should go downstairs now and take out the trash."

Jason wrapped his arms around her. "We didn't travel across the country to hide in your bedroom."

"Stop making sense!" Miranda pinched his butt for good measure. "Come on, werewolf. Let's go play nice."

CHAPTER THREE

When the group pulled up in front of Jessica's house that night, the peppermint odor was so strong that Jason stumbled near the front stoop. Peppermint had been the favorite treat of John Coleman, one of the White Coat scientists who tortured him in the lab. No matter how much Jason wanted to help Miranda make things right with her family, he would not easily get over that particular aversion.

Two big Dobermans raced out the front door to greet him in his state of disorientation. The dogs jockeyed for scratches and attention, which oddly made Jason feel a little more grounded to the reality around him, instead of his dark memories.

Miranda rushed to his side and put her arm around him. "Are you okay?"

"Peppermint like a sledgehammer to the face," Jason whispered as he patted the good dogs and shored his defenses.

With the full moon bearing down upon him, Jason's instinct was to tear his clothes off, shift into his wolf skin, and run as far away from the peppermint odor as possible. The Dobermans would probably run with him, which might be strangely fun. Not that he'd seriously entertain the notion in front of Miranda's family.

Acting out wouldn't help her, and Miranda definitely needed help. Her internal light had drained of its normal vibrancy as soon as she'd gotten in proximity to her family. The wrongness of it further added to Jason's feeling of unease.

The Christmas decorations were on full display for anyone entering the split-level ranch house. Monty, the oldest Lennox brother, lived there with his wife Jessica, their two children, and their Dobermans. Mitch, the second Lennox brother, and his wife Caroline were the proud parents of a boy and toddler twin girls. All the cousins could be heard playing with each other and the dogs.

Miranda had explained that she and her brothers all had the initials MCL because of their parents' names. The repeated M names, plus the brothers' similar appearance, made it confusing to keep everyone straight. It was one small grace that Jason wouldn't have to meet the third brother yet. Otherwise those baseball cards Miranda joked about would have been necessary for learning all the stats about Team Lennox.

Caroline swanned over to them to exchange opening pleasantries. After finding out Jason had grown up in Chicago, she said, "I have family there. Maybe we'll visit them when the kids are a little older. What about you? Do you get back there often?"

"No." Jason shook his head, skimming over any real talk of his past. "I live in New York now. That's where I met Miranda."

"Yeah. She went out there to study horses," Caroline said.

As observations about Miranda went, it was so basic that Jason couldn't tell if Caroline didn't know her sister-in-law very well or didn't have brain power for anything more in-depth.

The adults moved to the dining room, which was staged like a war council. Jason half-expected to see one of those poles for moving plastic soldiers from one combat theater to another. Instead of pieces for hypothetical war games, objects were strewn over the length of a full dining table, with ingredients to make into party favors on one end and photographs and personal memorabilia at the other end. Miranda planted herself there, looking through all the glimpses of her grandfather's past.

Malcolm "Pops" Lennox had been a poor Scottish immigrant. He and his wife Aileen, affectionately called Nan by all her grandchildren, met and fell in love on the ocean voyage. They built a good life for themselves, eventually settling in western Montana. Miranda's father, Michael, was the oldest of the Lennox sons born in the USA.

"Almost everyone will be at the party tomorrow," Caroline told Jason, "so you can meet them there. We have a few who won't be around until Christmas Day."

"Like who?" Miranda asked as she fingered an old photo on the table in front of them.

Caroline snatched the photo out of Miranda's hand as if she expected it to burn merely from skin contact with the fire shifter. Jason was unsure if the extended family was in denial or simply ignorant of Miranda's fire abilities. He had witnessed both Jessica and Christina snatch items away from her, but it was too soon to tell exactly why.

Jason had hoped to witness some latent sign of power in Miranda's nieces and nephews, but there was nothing obvious from what glimpses he'd seen so far. Everyone else in the house, from the oldest adult to the youngest child, seemed to be human without a single hint of being an energy shifter.

"Cousin Sean is bringing in a load of cars to sell at Mitch's dealership," Caroline said.

She seemed rather proud of her husband's job as management, but she never did specify what kinds of vehicle Mitch was selling.

"I won't be able to be there tomorrow, either," Jason said with an apologetic slumped pose. "I'm busy after sunset."

"It's a Jewish thing." Miranda lied so smoothly they could have rehearsed it ahead of time. Which they hadn't.

"You're Jewish?" With her eyes as wide as saucers, Caroline looked as if the possibility was shocking.

"My adoptive father is," Jason explained. "I'm exploring my thoughts on the subject."

It had only been a few days since Joel had extended the offer to make Jason a permanent member of the Rosen family. He now had a home with people who loved him without reservation. They'd start the paperwork after he and Miranda returned to New York.

"We'll still need you to help get everything ready," Jessica told him as she brought him a big mug of peppermint hot chocolate.

"No, thank you!" He shoved the obnoxious beverage away so forcefully it almost spilled. "I'm sorry! I hate peppermint."

"Really?" Jessica asked as if she couldn't imagine the possibility.

"I'm sorry," he repeated, moving to the other side of the combat theater.

Miranda's eyes followed him in sympathy. He quickly signed for her not to worry about it.

Monty strode into the dining room from the lounge where he'd put on a movie for the children. "I think we have an hour and a half. Tops. Let's do this while we can."

Mitch, leaning into his brother, whispered, "I have something to show you later. Our special calendar got delivered to the shop."

The brothers laughed, their hands in front of their faces.

Jason took a place at the table opposite Jessica and Christina to stuff bags and tie bows. Miranda stayed at the other end with Caroline to help make a collage—or she would, if the other woman would let her touch the materials. Pops was Miranda's grandfather, not hers, though Caroline didn't seem to take that into consideration.

As they separately worked on their tasks, the brothers and their wives made small talk about their day-to-day lives. Caroline told everyone about some of her recent sales achievements as a real estate agent. Jessica mentioned her involvement with her kids' school and the fundraiser she'd spearheaded. None of them asked Miranda what she'd done in New York or how her farrier course had gone. When Jason urged her with his eyes to say something, she stayed silent, only giving surly looks to everyone.

Miranda found her voice when she picked out a photo from the pile at the end of the table and showed it to Caroline. "This isn't Nan. I know Pops didn't have any sisters, so who's he holding like she's important?"

The two women studied the picture together, turning it over several times.

"It looks like her initials are CF. Whoever the mystery woman is," Caroline said, placing the photo back on the table, "she and Pops sure look lovey-dovey."

"Oooh. Pops had a secret girlfriend," Monty said.

Jessica playfully swatted his arm. "Did you ever have someone before me?"

"Wouldn't dream of it." Monty punctuated his statement with a kiss.

"Oh, wow. This is pretty cool. Pops used to be a volunteer firefighter!" Miranda said brightly. Then her expression morphed as she muttered to herself, "Did I know that and forget it?"

"There's a lot of stuff to know about a man who lives to be eighty," Monty said sagely. "I wouldn't sweat it."

"You kind of have to when you're putting together a timeline of the man's life. And loves. Maybe," Miranda said, flashing the picture of CF again.

An hour later, well before the movie ended, the children and dogs ran into the dining room on a mission of noisy chaos. Above the excited din, Caroline yelled that they'd knocked photos and memorabilia off the table.

"I think I can help with this," Jason said.

He stood from his chair and made the fingers to his eyes motion at each of the five running children. The fact that he was a stranger to them made the novelty factor work in his favor. Using Sign Language only to give them directions, he lured them out of the dining room and back to the lounge where the movie was glitching. The curious children followed him like ducklings.

Taking inspiration from Miranda's study of ASL fairy tales, he decided to sign them a story. He plopped down on the floor and motioned for them to do the same. After they joined him, Jason began signing the story of the *Three Little Pigs*. He audibly laughed to himself because Miranda had pointed out that the sign for "pig" reminded her of the hairs on the chinny-chin-chin.

Though they all watched, Riley, the seven-year-old daughter of Monty and Jessica and the oldest of this set of cousins, cottoned on to what he was doing faster than the others. As she recognized the stories, she said the words to match his signs out loud. Then the others joined in, alternately speaking the parts they knew or trying to copy his signs. Jason took the time to model the correct motions, so by the end of the story all the children were copying something.

Keeping the energy going, Jason next signed *Little Red Riding Hood*. That amused his werewolf sensibilities the most. It must have been a silent signal for Miranda to come out of the dining room to sit beside him. She gave him flirty eyes as she made the hand gesture for "wolf," and things were right in their world for a few seconds.

"Another one!" shouted Molly, one of Mitch and Caroline's twin daughters, when he'd finished the tale.

Her parents expected that others would not be able to tell the twins apart easily, but to Jason, the sisters had scents that were familial but clearly separate.

Jason looked intently at each of the children before him. [Do you want a Christmas story?]

Miranda asked him, "Do you know "Twas the Night Before Christmas'?"

"I have that story!" Oliver, Riley's five-year-old brother, shouted as he jumped up and ran out of the room. Faster than expected, he returned with a picture book and threw it on the floor in front of Jason like he'd made a touchdown.

[Thank you,] Jason modeled for the boy several times until he could repeat it.

"I'll read, and you can sign," Miranda suggested as she took the book to share the pictures with the children.

That worked just fine for Jason. They hadn't done this before, but it was a good partnership. He couldn't help smiling at her when he wasn't concentrating on signing the story in the most exciting way possible.

Before they reached the end, the phone in Jason's pocket started ringing, giving him a jolt. The children laughed at the way he jumped, but he decided to take the call. Less than ten people had his number, so it was likely someone Jason wanted to talk to.

He turned the face of the phone over to see it was from Lurlene, who was the best woman in the world in Jason's estimation.

"Mom!" he shouted into the phone, making the kids laugh and find their yelling voices after being quiet for a fairly long time.

"You didn't call me to tell me you'd arrived safely," Lurlene chastised.

"I'm fine. We're fine. We just got busy. I didn't mean to make you worry." Being a son of a good mother was a learning experience he hadn't expected. After a moment's hesitation, Jason said, "Let me talk to you outside. I need a break from all this peppermint."

Miranda stood to go with him, but she was called back to the dining room by Caroline.

"I need your help finishing the collage."

After a put-upon sigh, Miranda called out, "You don't want me to help you. You just want me to admire you while you do everything."

An accurate assessment as far as Jason was concerned.

Before he could go far, Miranda leaned closer to his phone. "Love you, Lurlene!"

"Love you, too, sugar," she replied.

With his phone back to his ear, Jason listened to Lurlene's updates about the family. He navigated an obstacle course of pets and people get to the kitchen, where Mitch and Monty were looking at a glossy calendar open on the countertop.

"So, how are you?" Lurlene asked with her soft Georgia drawl. "I had to make sure you were okay before I went to bed."

"Yeah, I'm—"

Mitch playfully jabbed him with his elbow and pointed at the calendar. "Who do you think is the sexiest?"

Jason was momentarily thrown off his train of thought, but he followed the pointing finger to photos of women in body paint posed as cars. The art was clever, and the women were beautiful.

But sexy? Well, his opinion on that was skewed by the pull of the full moon on his blood.

What Jason really wanted was a good fuck, preferably a good bottoming with a mind-blowing climax. Considering his partner's natural equipment, he was not likely to get such a thing without the aid of toys.

Glancing at the pictures again, he saw a man in the background of one of the photos holding up one of the women contorting herself with the other models into the appearance of a sports car. The man had nipple piercings and hair long enough to pull.

Without hesitation, Jason tapped on the man's chest. "Him."

Then he continued to the entryway where he slipped on his shoes and coat. The Dobermans joined him at the back door and walked out beside him.

Jason let out a deep sigh and breathed in the fresh air. Then he got back on the line with Lurlene. "Sorry about that."

"It sounds hectic over there."

"Yeah. Her grandfather's eightieth birthday is tomorrow." Jason ran his fingers through his hair and paced. "They're throwing him a big party. At night."

A beat came and went before Lurlene said, "But there's a full moon tomorrow night."

"Yes, that's the problem." He petted one of the dogs flanking his side as he walked and talked. "Miranda told them I couldn't be there for Jewish reasons, but that might not be enough."

"And how is Miranda really?"

"Putting on a brave face. I don't know what's going on here yet, but I don't like how they treat her." He exhaled and watched his breath turn into smoke. "It's not as bad as I had growing up in Chicago, but it's not good."

"Just because it's not bad," Lurlene said with a sad weight to her voice, "doesn't mean it can't be better. It's okay to ask more out of life. Be there for her if she needs it. Let her pick how that happens."

He nodded, though they weren't on a video call, and absently scratched the dog's ears again. "Wise advice."

Lurlene let out a loud yawn. "I must get to bed now. Call me on Monday after you're done with the full moon. Let me know you're okay."

"Maybe Miranda can do it while I'm still changed. Then I could howl into the phone for fun."

She chuckled. "Some other time, my silly boy. Love you."

"Love you, too, Lurlene. Tell everyone I already miss them."

He ended the call feeling much better. The fresh air had also helped cleanse the peppermint from his nose. Jason called the dogs to him and headed back inside the house.

As he walked through the kitchen, Monty and Mitch stared at him as if he had alien antennae coming out of his head.

"Which one did you think was the sexiest?" Monty asked.

"Him." Jason pointed again. It wasn't like there'd been many men there for him to focus on.

"Are you gay?" Monty asked.

At the same time, Mitch asked, "Does that mean you suck dick?"

"Well, sure, I do," Jason said to Mitch's question. "Don't you?"

"No! I'm not gay, you freak," he answered as if his very masculinity was threatened.

Jason couldn't help but let out a grin that might be described as wolfish. "Try it. You might like it."

Monty had a distasteful scrunch to his face. "I doubt it. I'm straight."

"Oh, that must be it." Jason snapped his fingers and shrugged. "I'm not. Ask a question, get an honest answer."

He pushed past them into the dining room. Miranda, still by Caroline's side, rolled her eyes and shook her head when she saw him.

Her brothers followed like a pair of hyenas ready to destroy. Mitch started first with a mocking laugh to all the adults present. "Miranda couldn't get herself a real boyfriend. She brought home a gay guy!"

"The gays are some of my best clients!" Caroline aimed a dazzling, if vapid, smile at Jason.

Jessica looked back and forth, from Mitch to Miranda. "She did what?"

"That's not what's going on." Miranda's gaze flitted to all of them as if willing them to understand.

"He's gay." Monty gestured at Jason.

"I'm not. You assumed," he corrected.

"He admitted he sucks dick," Mitch told everyone, directing his laughter in Miranda's direction. "Are you really so desperate to impress us with your success back east that you had to get a gay guy to be your fake boyfriend?"

Miranda looked mortified by her brothers' contemptuous accusations. Though Jason wanted them to eat their words, he crossed the dining room with a quick stride and wrapped her in his arms. He could endure abuse if necessary because that was the life he'd known until only recently. But this casual cruelty assassinated Miranda's character.

When the jeers subsided, Jason released the hug and pushed Miranda behind him, a wall of protection between her and everyone else. The disdain he felt toward them would make it easy to pop a wolf claw or elongate a fang without the rest of the transformation.

"You are all horrible. Don't you *dare* use me as a tool to hurt Miranda!" His voice roughened as he reined in his anger. "I have never hidden who I am from her. It's not our problem if *you* don't understand that!"

Miranda's arms encircled his waist as she pressed her face into his back.

"Well, how do I know you're not secretly lusting after me?" Monty asked with a snicker.

"I don't want you. But if we want to talk about secret lust, how about the way *your* pheromones went off the charts as soon as you looked at your brother's wife. Your own wife is ovulating right now. Maybe you should attend to that!"

The various adults shouted at Jason or stood up and knocked over chairs. He calmly held up his hand and said with quiet menace, "I've got more where that came from. I can go around this table and tell all your secrets and lies. Like the one of you who had a little too much alcohol today and the other one of you who needs to go to the doctor because you have a heart arrhythmia. I can hear your heart galloping, and it's not the sound of fear. But I do know what that sounds like."

Jason tromped out of the dining room to avoid Miranda's brothers and sisters-in-law. It was much easier to watch the animated movie with the children. He hadn't guessed he'd get this worked up, especially concerning his sexuality, which he'd never hidden. The better part of valor for Miranda's sake was to cool down so he wouldn't say anything else he might regret later.

Miranda quietly joined him and curled under his arm. He kissed her hair a few times, but they didn't speak or sign. Jason was now looking forward to the full moon where he could let himself go without worrying about what he ought to do. This time, his shift promised relief from his pent-up emotions.

CHAPTER FOUR

Miranda smoothed down the waist of her fitted blue and white clan tartan dress as she stood in the community hall the next day. The family had rented it for the birthday party on December 23rd, a date full of prime holiday party competition. All around her, family and friends buzzed to clean and put decorations in place. Jason had the deck broom and was putting his full moon energy to work. No dust mite would be left unslain.

They hadn't talked much after leaving Monty's house. Her brothers' taunts had been an unexpected gut punch. She was angry at them for saying such utterly stupid things about Jason and their relationship, and she was angry at herself for being ambushed by their words. Jason had defended her, but Miranda had taken their taunts without a fight as if that kind of treatment was okay.

Had she been part of her own abuse because she hadn't stood up for herself when she was younger? Some fights were so repetitive they wore a person down. And sometimes people believed their own bad press out of habit because it wasn't clear there were other options.

It was a new day, though, and Miranda would finally see Pops. She wanted him to be proud of her. She was no longer intimidated by the scope of her power. Her fire control could be big and bold or tiny and precise if needed. She'd come a long way from keeping horses warm in the barn as a little girl.

Her cousin Sheena stood, tapping her bottom lip with her index finger, in front of the photo collage timeline of Pops's life. The expression on her face looked critical.

"What do you think of it?" Miranda asked her as they stood side by side.

"Who made it?" Sheena asked quietly.

"Caroline with a little help from me. Mostly Caroline, because she thinks she's the best at everything since she's a real estate agent." No, she didn't sound bitter. Except she totally did.

"You know I love true crime, right? I've made murder boards that look better than this. I'm not impressed."

It was nice to hear someone else say it instead of Miranda. "You are a perfectionist, Sheen."

"Doesn't make me wrong," her cousin said. "I should go set up my station."

"Wait a sec," Miranda said with her hand on Sheena's arm. "We found something odd yesterday. A few odd things, actually. Do you remember much about Pops being a member of the volunteer fire department?"

"A little," she replied with a shrug. "Dad took us to the fundraisers when we were kids. I remember getting to sit on the fire engine."

"Do you know much about the night Pops burned his hand?" Miranda held her left hand in sympathy for the one her grandfather had damaged. "Was he answering a fire call?"

Shaking her head, Sheena said, "I have no idea. Not a clue."

"I was hoping you'd remember." Her cousin had been ten or eleven when the church burned. "You want to see something else we found?"

"If you make it quick." Sheena pointed to the booth she still had to put together.

Miranda pointed to the one of Pops hugging a young, fashionably dressed woman whose initials might be CF. "Looks like a girlfriend he probably had before Nan."

"People have exes all the time." Sheena didn't roll her eyes, but her tone implied it.

"It just stuck out, okay? Pops never talks about anything personal in Scotland before he came here. Blank slate. But secretly he's had a photo on him from sixty years ago? It's odd, if nothing else."

"Now you're sounding like one of my favorite podcast hosts. You could be on to something." Sheena nodded as if impressed. "Okay, gotta put everything together now."

Her cousin made a beeline to her party station, and Miranda gave one more look at the timeline. She could ask any of the firefighters who'd worked with Pops, assuming they showed up. Considering her grandfather's age and standing in the community, it was a party for everyone, not just the family.

While Miranda was wool-gathering, Nan spotted her and strode confidently across the expansive floor to greet her. Aileen Lennox was slightly older than Pops at eighty-two, but she was spry enough that Miranda could imagine the youthful charm her grandfather would have seen when the two met on their Atlantic crossing.

"Hi, Nan," Miranda said.

"That's a love." She hugged Miranda close. Nan always had good hugs for her, even in the bad times. Miranda should have spent more time with her. Maybe her childhood would have been less miserable.

"You've grown into a beautiful young woman." Nan ran her hand over Miranda's hair, flowing in loose waves down her back. "I remember when you were a wee bairn. My, how things have changed!"

"I would hope so! I am nineteen now," she said, feeling a blush rise on her cheeks.

"You were always a hot baby. Never kept your blanket on. Couldn't keep your socks on, either." Nan stepped back and patted Miranda's dress approvingly. "I was worried your mother wasn't feeding you properly when so many of your bottles of milk curdled. I don't know if the formula your mother got was spoiled, but you still became a beautiful young woman."

"Thank you," Miranda said, clutching her grandmother's hand.

Nan lifted her other hand to cover her next words. "Michael tells me you brought a young man home with you."

"Yes. The one with the deck broom over there." Jason lifted his head and waved his fingers at them. "He can't stay for the party, but he can meet Pops on Christmas Day."

Focusing on the most important thing, Nan asked, "Is he good to you?"

"He is. Very," Miranda said, pleased with a question about his character. "It's easy to be with him. He makes me feel... at peace."

Nan nodded. "It's not always like that. When I first met your grandfather, he was a very jealous man. I broke him of it because you do not sass a Scottish woman."

"No, you do not!" Miranda giggled with a conspiratorial incline of her head. Then she hooked arms and walked Nan over to the timeline collage. If anyone knew about Pops's past, it should be her grandmother.

"Caroline and I put this together. Everything we had from when Pops met you on the boat until now. I want to ask you about one of the photos." Miranda tapped the photo she'd already shown Sheena. "Do you know who this woman is?"

Nan took a long breath and stood taller. "I think that was Clara. He never talked about her very often, except for a few muttered words with his nightmares."

Maybe Pops had nightmares about saving her from the church. Miranda still dreamed of the terror of it all. On some nights, she was a crying mess, comforted only by Jason's arms.

"Was he saying Claire?"

Nan tilted her head to the side like an owl sizing up its prey. "No, dear. These were old nightmares, from before you were a twinkle in Michael's eye. We both have secrets we left behind, and I did not try to discover his."

Miranda would have had raging curiosity in Nan's place, but Jason, like Pops, had his own secrets. She didn't ask because she expected carnage. The suspicions he had confirmed already left her wondering how the werewolf wasn't a gibbering mess.

He walked over to her after finishing his task with the broom, and Miranda slid her arm around his waist. "This is Jason. He plays classical violin."

"When I have thumbs," he added perversely.

Nan looked at him askance. "Do you sometimes *not* have thumbs?"

"Sometimes I don't." He nodded gravely.

"How... peculiar," Nan said, then waved over their shoulders to someone on the opposite side of the room. "There's your cousin Sheena with the photo station. I need to speak to her."

After Nan left, Miranda pinched Jason's butt. "How long do we have until moonrise?"

"Not long. I'm... miserable."

He was sweatier than usual, and Miranda doubted it was because he'd recently been cleaning. Like her, Jason came with a higher body temperature, but this was different than normal. Granted, this was only their third full moon together.

"I thought your changes weren't painful."

"They aren't." He winced. "But I'm suffering in other ways."

She stepped into his personal bubble. "What ways?"

He flushed and turned his head. "Horny ways."

"Is this what werewolf blue balls look like?" She couldn't help the eruption of giggles, but she tamped them down as best she could. "I mean, you told me how you get around the full moon, but this is kind of funny."

"Not to me."

Miranda put her hand on his hip and stepped close enough to feel his discomfort. It gave her perverse pleasure. "Why don't you give yourself a hand and write something interesting in the snow?"

Jason's tone was flat and devoid of amusement. "I'd rather not."

Someone would take him back to the house soon, and he'd shift into his wolf skin to ride out the rest of the full moon. Miranda could take advantage of her boyfriend before he left. As long as he was willing, of course.

"Let's do something about it."

Taking his hand, she led him to the coat closet where her purse was hidden away. Miranda hadn't banked on needing any condoms, but in general she was usually prepared. The closet had a single lightbulb on the ceiling, and she pulled the long chain to turn it on. Then Miranda reached over to lock the closet door from the inside.

She held up the packet. "Hard and fast. Are you okay with that?"

"Yeah, I can do that."

The sound of his whimper was so pitiful that Miranda caressed his face before making fast work of liberating his penis from his pants. He leaned back against the wall, staring at the ceiling as she gave a few confident strokes. She had to restrain her giggle at how responsive his body was.

The logistical problem was how to get his parts touching hers. She would not settle for giving him a quick hand job or a blow job. Growling her own frustration, Miranda slipped off the pretty shoes she'd worn with her dress and slid the underwear down her legs, hiding them in her purse.

Jason gave himself a few strokes while he studied her, his pupils blown wide in the darkened closet. Then Miranda climbed him like he was her favorite tree. Together they worked so that his hard length was thrust inside her in one go. He held her to him with a grip low on her hips, and she squeezed him with her legs, rubbing her clit against him.

In their sexual encounters so far, Miranda was usually the aggressor. This time, perhaps influenced by the passion of the full moon itself, Jason took the lead. He changed their position so Miranda's back was pressed against the wall. Then, with hot and quiet words against her neck, he thrust into her again and again until his body stiffened. Miranda held him tighter, her orgasm on the edge of making an appearance, but when Jason stopped, it evaporated like dew under the morning sun.

"Did you?" he asked with a guilty expression.

Miranda shook her head. It would have been nice, sure, but the quickie had been for his benefit. Jason had not received the same memo. He dropped to the floor to worship her with his mouth until she was seeing stars. Miranda hadn't expected to come, but she buried her hands in his thick hair as intense pleasure rippled through her body.

In the aftershocks, Jason rubbed at his eyes as if still pained by the moon. Guilt wrapped around the pleasure of the orgasm. If Jason had stayed in New York, he could have had his transformation in peace instead of being an accessory to her family drama. Before she could apologize, the door handle jiggled, and Miranda was never more thankful that she'd locked it.

"It's Caroline," Jason whispered as he removed the condom and tucked himself back in his pants. "She's taking me back to your parents' house."

"Well, good for her," Miranda said. "She found you."

They both finished straightening their clothing, and Miranda flung open the door. "Caroline! Imagine meeting you here."

The woman jumped with surprise, giving them classic fish face while she searched for her words. Mitch appeared at his wife's side as if summoned by mischief. He did a double take, from Miranda to Jason, before he burst into mocking laughter.

"Is this what you do to prove he's not gay? Have sex in a closet so we'll catch you and believe you're a *real* couple?"

The idiotic comment nearly rendered Miranda speechless. Jason was much faster on the draw.

"I dunno about that." He handed Mitch the tied-off condom. "Here. Take this."

Mitch must have reached for it automatically, because he let out a manly shriek two seconds later and violently threw it aside.

He erupted in profanity so intense it made a few of the younger cousins walking by them run for cover.

"You are absolutely disgusting!" Mitch pointed at them and fought his gag reflex. "No wonder no one likes you!"

Their behavior clearly hadn't earned Miranda any points, but she'd never really been a family member in good standing anyway.

"I have to go now," Jason whispered in her ear. He lightly squeezed her arm and approached Caroline submissively. "Can you take me back to the house, please?"

Caroline continued to look flabbergasted but then pointed into the closet. "That's why I'm here. I need my coat."

"Oh, let me grab it for you." Miranda put on the biggest innocent helper smile she could manage.

Mitch was still enraged. "You should walk for that stunt!"

"Why would we walk when we can use one of the awesome cars from your dealership?" Miranda figured it best to appeal to her brother's sense of professional pride. "You said we should never waste free advertising."

Mitch didn't have a retort for that, but he spun on his heel, both middle fingers to the air as he marched away from them.

Before Caroline could take Jason away, Miranda flashed him the [I love you] sign over her heart. He mirrored it to her before disappearing. Hopefully he'd pass the rest of the night in peace.

After Jason left, it took nearly two more hours to get the community center ready because it was so full of activities. Cousin Sheena finished her photo booth with a green screen program. People could take photos as if they were in various parts of Pops's life. Uncle Ronald, Sheena's dad, put together a game of chance in one corner with Aunt Nancy. A bluegrass and folk band, comprised of several of the musicians Pops used to play with, warmed up in the opposite corner. As parties went, the different activities made the celebration a huge community blowout.

And of course, there was the cake. It was a multi-layered behemoth one might expect at a wedding, decorated with edible embellishments in blues, grays, and silvers. Instead of wax numbers at the top, it had eighty individual candles situated on the different tiers.

Miranda looked at it cross-eyed. She could light all the candles with nothing more than a thought, but it would be labor-intensive for anyone else on cake duty. It wouldn't be her. The immediate family never gave her anything to do that showed obvious connections to fire.

"Whose idea was that?" Miranda asked her mother, who was rushing by with a punch bowl.

"Some of your cousins, I think."

"Did they really think that was a good idea?" She held her left wrist and posed her hand into the deformed claw shape. "Give him a little PTSD for his birthday. It's the trauma that keeps on giving!"

Christina shook her head. "You think you can do better?"

"I think I can light all those candles without touching a match." Miranda waved her fingers in the general direction of the cake. "I'd hate to find out one of the cousins was just like me this whole time when I spent my whole life thinking I was the only one."

Her mother's eyes widened at the idea that there could be others in the Lennox family who could control fire. Maybe it was as intrinsic to the Lennox clan as the red hair. Without comment, Christina scurried away to finish her mission with the punch bowl.

Miranda asked several cousins about the cake. It was another of Sheena's projects, which made sense. Sheena was a natural entrepreneur with a hustle to be admired.

"Sheen, those candles are a fire hazard waiting to happen. Let me light them, and I swear everything will be okay," Miranda said. "I can do it without wrecking your beautiful cake."

"Girl, I was going to light them."

"But what if Pops doesn't have enough breath to blow them out?"

Sheena quirked her lips. "I hid a blow dryer underneath the table. It's a good joke, right?"

Yeah, it was, but Miranda still wanted to contain the candles. "Let me do it, and you can take the pictures."

Sheena took a few seconds to think about it. When she'd come to her conclusion, she tried to give Miranda the candle lighter.

"I don't need it." A smile curved Miranda's lips. "Just tell me when."

Applause preceded her grandfather's entry into the hall when he finally arrived. A few of the guests had party hats and noisemakers. He waved his good hand to everyone like he was royalty, but he was dressed as a commoner in jeans and a knit sweater, his faded hair neatly trimmed. Pops looked healthier at eighty than some of the younger men around him.

Miranda wanted to rush over and hug him. And tell him about all the progress and self-discovery she'd made in New York. She controlled her fire. The fire didn't control her. It wasn't a burden or danger to anyone.

When he got to her, time almost stood still. Here was the man she'd loved with all her little girl heart, who made music that she'd danced to. She'd been so happy as a child with her grandparents, but when the people at the church tried to squelch her fire like exorcising a demon, he had been the one to pay for it. It had been a wonder that he was able to get there in time to save her from the evil that strangers tried to do to her.

"I see you're back from New York." Pops had never been overly affectionate, so his flat statement was practically glowing.

"I am. I brought my boyfriend with me. You'll like him. He plays violin like you did." She smiled and hoped he'd see the connection.

He put his gloved left hand on her arm. "A lot of people do, lass. It's not special."

But it reminded me of you, and I liked that. "Right. Well, I'm back, and I need to talk to everyone after Christmas."

Miranda leaned in to hug him. He returned it, but with enough space that someone could have been standing between them. After releasing the hug, Pops continued greeting the people who stood in the informal receiving line. Disappointed, Miranda wandered off to the kitchen.

Her father stood pilfering appetizers while a few of the women continued the food setup. When they were alone, he said, "You look deflated."

"I wanted to talk to Pops. To tell him what I'd done. I'm proud of myself, Dad, but no one wants to hear that."

She put her hands on the counter, dropped her head, and sighed.

"You finished your education. Good for you. But you still need a job."

"I'll get a job when I go back to New York!" She snapped her head up in annoyance. "No, Dad. This is about the thing no one talks about. That I can set things on fire with my brain. I'm good at it. When I was in New York, I learned to do more things with it than ever before. I wasn't afraid of it, and people weren't afraid of *me* for merely existing beside them."

Michael frowned, shooting dark glances toward the door as he got so close to Miranda's face that she could see a small piece of meat stuck between his teeth.

"You can't ever speak about it with anyone! It's a danger to you and to the rest of us. It's unnatural. You shouldn't be able to do any of it."

"But I can," she replied, a tiny flame erupting from her lips as if she were a fire-breathing dragon.

"Stop it!" He raised his hand like he was going to slap her.

Miranda stood her ground. "It's just something I can do, Dad. If I was a singer with a beautiful voice, would you tell me to shut up and not sing? No, you wouldn't! You'd want me to take my talents and get better at using them."

"Is that what you did in New York? I thought you were shoeing horses."

With a confident smile, she said, "I can do that, too. And even if I did go to New York just to play with fire… so what? I went there on my own, paid for my education, and worked a job I got on my own merits. I made friends in New York, people who like *me*!"

"If New York was so great, why are you back here in Montana?"

She'd been struggling with a simple way to say what she wanted. Maybe there was no simple way.

"You, Mom, the boys… none of you act like you even like me. You might love me because that's what you're expected to do. But you don't *like* me." She scuffed her foot on the checkerboard tiles. "I deserve better than that. If I were a stranger, you wouldn't treat me so coldly. But I'm the one who gets the blame and all the jabs of verbal cruelty when things go wrong."

"No, you don't. That's enough." Michael crossed his arms and tapped his fingers on his forearm.

"I know a horrible thing happened when I was a little girl. And I can never apologize enough for defending myself. I was scared, Dad. And no one was there to help me! I would never have hurt anyone if they hadn't tried to hurt me first. You can't keep blaming me for that!"

Miranda wiped at the hot, wet tears that fell from her eyes.

"So you want an apology?"

"It would be a start. You don't know what it was like growing up feeling like everything you did was wrong."

Michael shoved away from the counter where he was leaning. "You've obviously never met your grandfather."

It was easy for her to forget sometimes that her father and his brothers had the pressures common to the first-generation children of immigrants. Yet his suffering didn't make hers excusable.

"I am strong and capable. None of you see me as I *am*, just as a pathetic but dangerous little girl frozen in time. I want you to see me and respect me!"

There. That was the essential nugget. It was a piece of the impossible. Miranda rubbed her hand over her face and sighed.

The kitchen door swung open, and Sheena stepped through. "Come on, Miranda! It's time to light the cake."

Miranda nodded and followed her cousin, keeping her eyes focused on Sheena's back.

"What do you mean, *light* the cake?" Michael demanded behind them.

"Exactly what you think, Dad," she replied with a dramatic flip of her wrist. "I promise to put on a good show."

CHAPTER FIVE

The band played something festive as the women approached the table. Pops stood by the cake, nodding and sometimes waving his undamaged hand. When his eyes fell on Miranda, his generally pleasant expression turned guarded. He stared at her while Sheena whispered in his ear about the blow dryer.

Standing slightly in front of Pops and Miranda, Sheena gave a short speech to the assembled crowd as she held her professional camera in her hands. Then she turned slightly to cue Miranda to light the candles.

As easy as breathing, Miranda sensed all eighty wicks of the candles and let them spring to life. Sheena goggled at her but took photos of the cake and Pops standing beside it. A few of the kids exclaimed how cool it looked while others demanded to know how the candle trick happened. Pops kept a fake smile for the crowd but shot Miranda a private glare when he turned his head.

"I bet they were all on a timer," one of the tween boys said confidently.

"Blow 'em out, Pops," cried a voice from the back.

Like a trooper, he took out the hair dryer, wielding it like a weapon to control the flames. He blew out all the candles while the band played the familiar melody of "Happy Birthday to You." The crowd cheered, and the old man held up the dryer, victorious.

Miranda, perhaps already drained of any of her good decision-making ability that night, let some of the candles spring back to life. It was only her amusement that guided the display. She alternated the flames as if they were electric blinking bulbs. Then she made bigger shapes in the mass of candles, taking inspiration from the holiday season to make the flames appear red and green.

The children around her enjoyed it enough to applaud and request different things for the flames to do. It was doubtful they knew that she was controlling the flames. But Pops did, and the old man looked ready to throw hands.

"That's enough!" His anger gave his voice a sharp edge. Pops shook the dryer at her as if to beat her, and Miranda put her hands in the air in surrender.

"Well! Wasn't that pretty entertainment with the candles?" Sheena said in the perfect hostess voice. "It's time to cut the cake and listen to some more music!"

Miranda stepped away, but before she could get too far, a hand clamped on her shoulder. She spun around to face both her father and grandfather.

"What did you *do*?" Michael asked.

"I lit the candles. Just like I told you I was going to do." She stared from one man to the other, both of them studies in anger.

"You can't keep haunting me, Clara!"

"Claire," she said sharply. "My name is Miranda Claire."

"Forget the name!" Michael clenched his jaw and lowered his voice. "You're not supposed to use your fire tricks. Did all those dead people and your disfigured grandfather teach you nothing?"

"More than you know," she whispered. "It taught me to feel ashamed of myself. But not once were the candles out of control."

"You vengeful witch!" Pops spat at her in a voice meant to carry no farther than her or Michael's ears. "I never want your hateful evil near me again. Don't you dare show up at the house for Christmas dinner. I don't want to see you!"

The old man shook with rage, and it was enough that even Michael said, "Dad?"

"You can't keep punishing me for something I did when I was five years old!" Miranda stomped her foot and tried her best to hold back her tears. "I've apologized for everything I've done, and I've learned to control my power. Why haven't you forgiven me?"

Whirling away from them before she really did start crying, Miranda grabbed her purse and jacket before seeking freedom outside. On the back steps of the community hall, she stared up at the stars and enjoyed the blazing full moon. She imagined going back to Jason and running free. It would almost be a good idea if shooting wolves wasn't some people's idea of sport.

A boot scuffing beside her a few seconds later made Miranda turn her head to a man in his mid-twenties trying to light a cigarette.

"Sean?" He wasn't supposed to be there until Christmas Day.

"Miranda? What are you doing out here, little cousin?" He opened his arms to give her a hug.

"I got in a fight with Dad and Pops," she said into the shoulder of his puffy winter coat.

"Was it about your new boyfriend and the quickie in the closet?"

She gaped when he let her go. "How did you know about that? Is the family grapevine that fast?"

"Nah." He laughed. "You forgot I work with Mitch. I brought the delivery in early, and he had to tell me *everything*. I mean, who doesn't like a hot bag of jizz for Christmas?"

Miranda closed her eyes, the mortification finally setting in. Sean didn't seem to notice.

"You got yourself one of them bisexual boys? That's one way to stick it to your parents."

"That's not why we're together."

"Okay." He didn't sound convinced and busied himself with trying to light his cigarette. "Damn it! So what were you and Uncle Mike fighting about then?"

She stared at her cousin and decided to take a leap of faith. Sean had always been one of those people all the cousins liked. A lot of fun with a kind word to most.

"This." Miranda held out her hand with a delicate flame rising above each finger.

Sean silently looked from her fingertips to her face and back again several times. "Is that real?"

"You're the one with the cigarette."

Gingerly, he touched it to the flame above her middle finger. When the tip of the cigarette glowed orange, Miranda shook her hand dramatically to show the flames going out.

Sean stared at the lit cigarette for a few seconds and then took a long drag. He changed his position so they were shoulder to shoulder looking up at the sky. She didn't speak, and he didn't ask until he was done smoking.

"You're the reason Pops can't use his hand, aren't you?" It was just a question. No obvious sounds of judgment attached to it.

"I am." Tears threatened to leak out of her eyes again, and she didn't want to cry.

"I'm sorry, Miranda. That's got to be tough."

She laughed. "Understatement!"

A few seconds later, Sean put another cigarette in her face. "Light me."

For fun, she blew out a breath that set the tip on fire. "Why aren't you freaked out about this?"

"Still trying to figure it out," he said with a shrug. "It's like some anime shit. Did it just happen one day, or…"

"It's always been a part of me. Nan just reminded me of what I was like as a baby, and yeah. My whole life." Miranda made eye contact to gauge if he was still listening. "I had a run-in with a geneticist in New York, and he thought I was the first of a brand-new genetic mutation. Other people might start having powers."

"I guess." Sean threw down the last of the cigarette and stepped on the ember with his heel. "Does it hurt you when you do your fire thing?"

Miranda opened her mouth to answer and then shut it. No one in her family had ever asked her that before. They wanted her to hide the ability, not encourage it with questions. There was something freeing about how easily Sean asked her about it.

"It used to give me headaches sometimes, but I was also trying to hide it." She wrung her fingers as she figured out how to describe it. "My boyfriend Jason loves it. He can see my aura and has encouraged me to embrace it all. He also makes sure I guzzle electrolyte drinks to keep my brain happy."

"Sounds like a good dude. Look forward to meeting him. So what kinds of things can you do?"

"Whatever my imagination wants! I can light things without touching them. I can put out fires, too. Not just little ones, either. I've gone into burning buildings and… poof! No more fire. And I can make pinpoint fires."

The previous weekend, Miranda had run into her kidnapper in public. She'd systematically burned the capillaries in his brain, forcing him into a stroke. Her anger burned deadly, but it wasn't mad and mindless. She still hadn't told Jason what she'd done.

"Well, I...," Sean said as he stepped into her personal space again, "think it's awesome. We could have gone on so many adventures when we were kids if I had known about it!"

"Like what?" Miranda asked as he enfolded her into a hug.

"Hot rodding and staying out all night."

She hugged him back because it was a relief to be accepted without conditions. "Wish I could do that now. I've got to get away from here."

"Your wish is my command." Sean pulled his keys out of his pocket and dangled them enticingly in the air. "Make sure you fill the tank before you give it back."

Miranda eyed the keys with hopeful hesitation. "You're going to let me drive your baby?"

"As long as you can drive stick, it's yours."

She snatched them from his hand. "Who did you think you were talking to?"

"Didn't want to assume. Not everyone knows how. Sheena doesn't."

"You just didn't want your sister to drive your car," she teased before giving him a quick hug. "Thanks, Sean."

"No problem," he said with a final squeeze. "See you soon, cuz."

Miranda dashed for the parking lot where she'd find his classic purple GTO. Next stop: picking up her werewolf boyfriend and hitting the road.

CHAPTER SIX

Bending low over the sleeping werewolf, Miranda marveled at how large he was. It made sense that Jason would follow the law of conservation of matter for his transformations, but a wolf shifter was significantly larger than a wolf in the wild. He'd curled himself in a ball to try to look small on the floor of her childhood bedroom.

She sat down in front of him and ran her fingers through his fur while she tried to regulate her emotions. After a minute that felt much longer, she put her forehead on top of his. He roused to wakefulness as she bathed him in her tears.

This was only the third time Miranda had been with Jason during the full moon, so she was still figuring out how it all worked. He wouldn't hurt her, though. His basic nature was gentle, a balm to her often aching spirit.

"It did not go well with Pops or my dad." Miranda wiped at the side of her face. "I don't want to be here when they get back. How do you feel about a moonlight road trip?"

He sat up and gave a soft yip. She smiled because he was still in there, even with a different face.

"Let me change my clothes. Then we'll go raid the fridge."

Pulling the tartan dress off and throwing it on the bed, Miranda reached for a clean pair of underwear, jeans, and a long-sleeved shirt. She added cotton socks and then went to the bathroom to brush her hair.

Down in the kitchen, Miranda found a small, portable cooler and put her electrolyte waters into it. Then she added meat and cheese slices and crackers, the makings of a charcuterie board in a fancier situation. Glancing around for any other things she might like, she swiped Jason's full pack of jumbo marshmallows.

"Let's hit it."

She carried her bundle to the door, stopping to take her mother's long red cloak off the hook. Christina had it set out because she was going to play Mrs. Claus with all the grandkids for Christmas. Lastly, Miranda also found a fleece blanket to put on the seat of Sean's car so Jason's claws wouldn't scratch the upholstery.

After locking the door behind them, Miranda trotted ahead to the car. She spread the fleece out on the passenger seat and waved her hand like a game show model for Jason to get in. The cooler full of snacks fit nicely on the floor in front of him.

Miranda got behind the wheel and drove with no particular place in mind. It wasn't like she had friends she could visit. She'd never found making friends an easy thing until she met Lisa, one of the other students in her farrier course. Lisa had done most of the work in showing her how to behave as a friend should.

She reached over to turn on the radio for some noise, but it couldn't drown out the pain she felt over a lifetime of rejection. Jason nuzzled her thigh with his long lupine nose. Miranda patted his head and steered with her left hand.

"I don't know why I'm here, Jason. I could have stayed in New York and been fine."

It had been her idea to face her family, but maybe she had only bad ideas. It wasn't that she thought coming back would automatically fix everything. She just hadn't realized that she'd have to keep standing up for herself, that there would be no time when she'd be done with it all.

Maybe she should have gotten a clue from unabashedly queer Jason and Lisa, who was a proud bisexual. Though Miranda was straight, they'd shown her by how they lived that there was a continual coming out process.

If Miranda wanted people to know her ability, she'd have to tell them about herself over and over. Or she could stop using her fire and pretend to be someone she wasn't. But what kind of life was that? Not one she wanted, that was for sure!

She drove through parts of the county that she hadn't seen in ages and over country roads laden with snow. Miranda wasn't so removed from Montana that she'd forgotten how to drive cautiously. An idea struck her, perhaps inspired by winter surrounding her as it had so long ago. Her new mission was to find the ruins of the old church.

It had been a wooden building with humble clear windows instead of the stained glass of some of the fancier churches. The baptistry was tucked behind the pulpit. It had been a rather pretty church in its prime. If it could have been recreated, it would have been a perfect frontier movie set. The beauty of it existed only in memories now.

As Miranda parked near the burned husk of the old church almost an hour later, she noted that nothing new had been built on the grounds in the years since her accident. It was still a charred wasteland.

[We're here,] she signed. This place didn't need to be disturbed by her voice. She'd already done that by screaming herself raw as a child.

After she opened the door for Jason, he hopped to the ground with its light dusting of snow. The werewolf stood breathing in the winter night, plumes of steam coming from his mouth, turning his head this way and that as he studied the remains of the building.

Together, they cautiously crossed onto the grounds that did not have any snow cover. Though peculiar, that didn't mean they were walking on holy ground, even if young Miranda had bathed it in primordial fire akin to an Exodus story.

Coming home had made her realize that her memory of the kidnapping was spotty at best. How had she been stolen away to the church in the first place? Her parents were not regular attendees of anything in particular. They'd moved to a different part of the county after she'd burned this church down. Not a full new start, but something extreme enough that her brothers had to go to new schools. They'd complained about missing their friends because of their sister.

Miranda had never meant any harm when her fire first came out. It was as normal to her as the babbling that babies did when they first learned to talk. She had used her ability to comfort cold animals in Pops's barn. Her heart had been kind once. Miranda wasn't sure it still was.

At the edge of what had been the building's frame, Jason lifted his lupine head, making a show of inspecting the burned beams. He stepped around Miranda and pawed a hymnal with some of the pages still intact, though faded and damaged by the elements.

He returned to Miranda, still standing outside the frame, and leaned against her thigh. She sighed at his quiet support and found her voice.

"When I got to high school, I looked up the names of everyone who died here. I know them all. Sometimes I mourn for every one of them and how senseless it was."

She kicked the floor as they walked in. "Sometimes I curse them for trying to hurt me and being willing spectators. I was a child! All I wanted was to be safe with my family. All children want to be safe and loved. I... was not."

Her brothers ignored her. Hugs from her parents became fewer. Miranda was the monster who lived in the Lennox house. She'd often wondered if they would have been happier if she'd died in the church, a victim of her own power. Maybe they just wanted her ability to go away, to trade in their defective daughter for someone else they could understand.

Jason's trust in her, though, helped her to get to a place of self-acceptance. She had people back east, like Lisa and the Rosen family, who knew what she could do and treated her fire control as intrinsic to her as the fact that she had brown eyes.

The werewolf let out a soft croon, and Miranda put her fingertips in his thick fur. She still wondered where all the hair went when he returned to his human-looking shape. She supposed she'd never find out.

As if dragged by an overwhelming current over a waterfall, Miranda gave in to the pull of the baptismal font. Images of her ordeal, which had been long hidden, rushed back to her like smoke. There'd been so many people in the church that night. The noise and the shouting seemed to all be directed at her. Then people put hands on her, and that was something her parents had told her to never accept.

She'd been confused. Wasn't her grandfather there? His face flickered in and out of her memory, like a glitch in her matrix. The priest or preacher or whatever he was wrestled her away from the others. Then he shoved her under the water, his hands manacles on her body. He would not let her up! She flailed and struggled, but they were going to drown her. If she was left for dead, would her brothers or her parents know?

Doing the only thing she could do, Miranda had sent a burst of fire out in all directions. They had to stop touching her and let her go! Then she heard the loud voices change to screams of terror. She wanted the voices to stop. Just stop! So she pressed out another wave of fire to take everything in its wake. Someone else touched her, and Miranda didn't know if it was yet another person trying to extinguish her living fire. She latched on and burned with feral rage. Through the haze of the fire, she saw Pops there to save her from all the people who wanted to cause her harm.

She cried and limply went into his arms. By then, the damage to him had already been done. No more would Malcolm Lennox be the most renowned fiddler in northwest Montana.

Snapping out of the memory, Miranda looked around the skeleton of the once lovely building. The winter moonlight that bathed it all in beauty could not drive away the destruction in her past.

Jason leaned against her again before loping off to inspect the area, loudly sniffing everywhere. He whimpered as he looked up to the sky and trotted back to her.

Miranda bent down and hugged his neck, new tears falling down her cheeks. "I won't find any answers here. Everything is dead."

She picked her way over the ground until they were outside what had been the foundation. Miranda turned back for a final look. With no more effort than a sigh, she burned the remains of the structure, hot and fast, until it was merely ash floating in the winter night like a perversion of snow.

"I have marshmallows in the car. Come on."

She opened the door for him to climb in and then dug around the cooler for snacks. Taking out a fat marshmallow, she burned it to perfection at the tips of her fingers. Jason studied her intently, so Miranda gave him the same regard.

"Can you even taste sweet things in this form? Dogs can't eat chocolate, and cats don't have the tastebuds for sweetness."

When he gave an upward nod, she shrugged. "It's your fur."

Flaming a big marshmallow for him, she set it at his open mouth. The maw of teeth, so huge and feral, could have scared her if she hadn't known the werewolf within. He tipped his head back and worked the marshmallow with his long tongue, and the silliness of it all made Miranda smile.

She took his paw, running her thumb over his claws and his cute wolfy toe beans. His presence comforted her, but Miranda was also ridiculously fascinated with Jason's body, whether he appeared as a man or a wolf. It was still all him.

After a few more marshmallows for both of them, Miranda sighed. "Life wasn't the same after the fire. My parents moved and uprooted our lives. Even my grandparents moved. To get away from the damage and shame maybe. But I was still with them. Their personal albatross."

She let go of Jason's paw and put her hands around her waist under the cloak. "I already loved horses. They were the reason I showed my power in the first place. But then I loved *only* horses because... my family didn't even like me. They were scared and acted like I was a devil child from a cheap horror movie from the '70s."

While she was lost in her memory, Jason tapped the cooler with his forepaw with enough intensity that she opened the lid for him. He poked his nose into it and lifted a bottle out with his teeth. Miranda took it from him, noting that it was the electrolyte water that he insisted she drink after fire manipulation.

She wiped the bottle cap off with the cloak and patted his furry head. Then she leaned forward and placed a kiss between his eyes.

Resting her forehead against his, she said, "Thank you for always thinking of me."

Miranda then took a long pull from the bottle and stared at the barren land. She'd wanted to come back to something better for herself. All she could reasonably say was that she'd been a child with no support. If there were others like her in the world, she wanted their lives to be better than hers had been.

Wiping her mouth with the back of her hand, she let out a noise that wasn't quite a burp. "All right. Time to head back. This is going to take a few hours."

They drove away, and Miranda had no intention of ever coming back again.

CHAPTER SEVEN

As they drove back to Miranda's parents' house, Jason reflected on what he'd learned at the site of one of Miranda's greatest traumas. His enhanced senses told him many things that her words could not. The air and the grounds of the church had been burning in the energy fields as if Miranda had permanently scarred the land as a child. Burning it all into an ash heap had only been the cap of that long-ago event.

Jason wondered if Miranda might burn so hot one day that she could turn herself into a phoenix to exist only as energy. Maybe when Miranda died. Not that he wanted that to be any time soon.

They neared the Lennox farm when it was very dark, right before the impending dawn. Jason was still under the full moon's pull, but the shape lock was almost complete. The catalyst for the original werewolf program had been stem cell research because the cells replaced themselves every month. Somehow it keyed into the werewolf's moon change so that in scientific theory and lived-in reality, he was a completely new person every twenty-nine and a half days. The thirteen-hour period was when the cells did their biological magic.

As Miranda parked the car, the noise of the change took over Jason's ears. The sensation of new stem cells taking over was an ambient hum in his neurons from snout to tail, ears to claws. The hum rose in internal volume and intensity. When Jason was a much younger werewolf, inexperienced in his shifts, he might have feared not being able to come out of a shift. The rest of his cohort had given themselves over to fear and madness. Jason, on the other hand, had learned to shift well and often, but he kept that talent hidden from the White Coats who'd regimented his life for seven years.

Sweeping her hand out as a guide for Jason to get out of the car, Miranda grabbed the blanket and small cooler. She patted him affectionately as she might do for a real beast and not her boyfriend, but he didn't complain. His attention was on the electricity within him. Not time yet. Soon.

Jason walked on silent paws in Miranda's shadow as she led them to the wrap-around porch. The bright red cloak billowing around her was quite the fetching sight. Less fetching and lovely were her parents, who rushed out the door in their sleeping clothes and slippers.

"Miranda Claire!" Michael Lennox twisted her name like a foul thing in his mouth. "Where have you been?"

"I went for a drive to clear my head." She put the cooler down in front of her and stood like a schoolgirl being reprimanded by teachers.

"And where is that boy you brought with you?" Christina demanded.

"He's twenty-four, Mom," Miranda shot back. "That boy is a man."

"That boy" was also currently wolf-shaped. But who was Jason to quibble? He wondered if he could sneak off to the barn to hide. It wasn't like he and Miranda had made a plan of how to reveal his lycanthropy or keep it completely hidden.

Christina gestured vaguely to Miranda's upstairs bedroom. "Whatever he is, he's not in the house, and you two were caught making out in the closet at the birthday party."

It was a little more than simple making out. The orgasm had been... needed. When Jason wore a different face, he might let himself feel embarrassed about that. Right now, though, Miranda's parents still hadn't noticed him, which was odd. He wasn't tiny by any estimation.

Michael took up the parental tirade next. "You think having a quickie in the closet makes you look anything less than easy?"

Miranda balked at that, and Jason had to restrain a growl on her behalf. "I think you told me not to have sex in your house. Technically, we didn't, and the only one who has a right to complain is Mitch."

"Damn it, Miranda!" Michael pounded his fist on the porch railing. "You spread your legs for anyone in the county and then bring home a stranger from New York who's just as cracked as you are. And you had the audacity... the gall to light the candles on the birthday cake."

"You upset your father and your grandfather," Christina said, an obvious assessment even to Jason who hadn't been there. "Does that boyfriend of yours know about your fire?"

He did, yes. Jason had first seen her across the room at a crowded frat party, and even if they'd never become a romantic couple, knowing Miranda had forever changed him.

Miranda stood taller, throwing back her shoulders. "He thinks it's beautiful."

"It is not beautiful. It's destructive and ruins lives," Michael said. "You need to forget you know anything like that and be a normal girl."

Miranda snarled at them. "If I'm not normal, it's because this is the way you made me. I came out of the womb like this. Not my fault. *You* did this!"

Michael started creatively swearing again and raised his hand toward Miranda. She flinched but did not back down. Jason didn't know if her father would actually strike her, but the protective part of him would not stand for it. It seemed that Michael and Christina Lennox were about to find out just what kind of man Miranda had brought home with her.

His voice full of lupine menace, Jason stepped out from behind Miranda, his shoulder bumping against her hip. Upon seeing him, Christina screamed and leaped into Michael's arms. Both of their body chemistries changed from scents of anger to fear.

"Get your gun, Michael. Get your gun!" Christina wailed with a voice that got higher and higher.

"No!" Miranda threw her body protectively over Jason. "Don't hurt him!"

"He's a monster!" Michael said, slowly backing away with Christina clinging to him.

"Dad, please!" She put her hand out as if to beg for patience. "There are things you don't understand. Let me bring him inside. We'll go to my room, and we won't bother anyone."

Still clinging to his wife, Michael said, "That... thing... is not coming inside my house!"

As father and daughter argued, the last of the full moon hum faded from Jason's body. He could voluntarily slip out of this shape. There was no reason to show Miranda's already terrified parents the truth of his existence, but maybe it would help these strangers to know that the world was much stranger than they thought. If he and Miranda were monsters, at least they could be monsters together.

He whined and tugged on the red cloak and tugged to get Miranda's attention.

"It's time?" she asked with a trembling whisper.

Jason snorted to confirm, and Miranda stood up, using her body as a shield between him and her parents. Then, with flair that would have been more appropriate for a theater kid than a horsewoman, Miranda drew the cloak from her shoulders and held it out to obstruct her parents' view of Jason's shift.

Using all the speed he possessed, Jason moved from the four-legged wolf to the two-legged man who'd escaped from the lab. He was used to the noise of his change, but Miranda winced as his bones and ligaments rearranged into a new form. So did her parents, who looked confused and ready to vomit.

When at last he could stand on his own five-toed feet, Jason took the cloak and wrapped it around himself. He fastened the closing brooch at his left shoulder, minimizing any naked skin on display, and shook out his blond mane.

"So... there are some things we need to talk about," Miranda said, though she avoided eye contact with her parents.

"Let me take a shower and get some breakfast first," Jason said, his voice a little scratchy from his shift. "Changing forms burns a lot of calories, and I need to eat. But I can answer your questions if you want to ask me anything."

Miranda placed her hand at the small of his back and propelled him forward, silently daring her parents to keep them out of the house now that they knew who the monster was. Michael and Christina shrank away from him as if lycanthropy was caused by an airborne pathogen.

———◉———

JASON FINISHED HIS shower in no time, a habit from years of needing to move quickly in case his past caught up with him.

After knotting the towel securely around his waist, he lathered up to shave.

Following a soft knock on the door, Miranda let herself into the bathroom. She closed the door and propped herself up on the countertop. He shifted his eyes in her direction, but he focused on shaving. The noise of the house loomed, and water rushed in the pipes, likely a shower in the master bath.

One side of his face done, Jason rinsed the razor blades and tapped the excess water on the sink basin. Then he began his slow, methodical work on the other side of his face.

[Maybe you need an electric razor for Christmas,] Miranda signed slowly. She was still building vocabulary, but Jason was proud of the progress she'd made in a short time.

"I don't think anyone's getting me anything for Christmas," he said. "But if they do, the running favorite is dog biscuits. Or condoms."

Miranda rolled her eyes, and Jason concentrated on the rest of his shave. He wiped his face off with a washcloth and inspected his work.

"You missed a spot."

She touched a particularly thick beard hair on his jaw with her fingertip. He lifted the razor, but she shook her head. In the mirror, a spark of flame from her fingertip took out the hair as easily as a dermatologist's laser.

He squinted at his reflection. No stray hairs remained. With a nod, he signed his thanks and splashed on some aftershave that had been a gift from Lurlene before they left Ithaca.

Miranda gestured for him to come back to her, so he stepped into the vee of her legs. She wrapped herself around him, clutching his body to hers. When she began to tremble, he pressed his lips to the side of her neck, near where her jaw met her ear. Holding his hips tight with her thighs, Miranda put her hands in his thick hair and kissed him like doing so was the only thing that gave her peace.

The friction of their bodies made the knot in the towel work itself out. Taking advantage of the opportunity, she clutched his ass, kneading the muscles there. Jason needed Miranda to try pegging him soon. But maybe not while they were still in Montana. It would only add to the scandalous reputation they'd developed in less than forty-eight hours.

He broke away from her kiss and paused. Jason had many secrets and a world full of trauma he had not yet shared with Miranda. But she had trusted him with the deep truth of her pain.

Jason took Miranda's hand, gently stroking each finger and studying her knuckles. "In the energy fields, the original fire around the church was still burning. Even before you finished the job. It looked like... a scar the land never forgot. A remnant like in some ghost tales."

Her fingers stiffened. When he looked up, Miranda's brown eyes flickered back and forth like she was figuring out her best response.

"You don't have to say anything. I know you can't see your aura the same way I do, but I thought you'd want to know."

"Is that... supposed to make me feel better?"

Jason shrugged. He didn't know. On some level, she had to be aware of the intensity of the power she possessed. It was her lived-in experience, after all. But what if she hadn't consciously known?

"It tells me they hurt you and were not kind."

Miranda sniffled and turned her head away. "Well, they're not going to be very kind to *you*. This is Montana where people shoot wolves for fun. You don't want someone's trigger finger to slip, and you sure don't want to get on the lab's radar again!"

"Even with my new identity, I know I'm only one false move from ending back at the lab." Jason wrapped his finger around one of her long, red tresses and tried to catch her eye. "But it doesn't matter. I had to show your parents."

Miranda slapped his hand away. "No, you didn't! I should have made sure the coast was clear or had you hide in the barn."

"What's done is done." He put his knuckles on the counter at the sides of her legs and leaned forward. "They're horrible when they talk to you. I wanted your parents, for once, to see you like I do. Maybe knowing you had someone in your corner would help them change their minds."

"They are not Joel and Lurlene." Miranda threw her hands out as if pointing to Jason's invisible parents. "You've put a target on your back."

"I always had one. The only thing that's changed is who's doing the shooting."

Miranda shook her head, and Jason took another kiss. Then he stepped back and held his hand out so she could hop down from the counter. Once both her feet were on the floor, Jason took the towel that had pooled around his ankles and put it on the rack to dry.

The two of them walked down to the kitchen after he got dressed. Miranda's parents hadn't made it there yet for the talk they needed to have, so she assembled a ham and cheese sandwich for each of them. Putting her hands above them like a stage magician with an illusion, Miranda toasted the bread to crispy, brown perfection.

"Amazing!" Jason cheered before taking his plate.

Michael and Christina entered the kitchen a few minutes later, showered and still looking pale from their lycanthropic encounter. They sat down at the table opposite him and Miranda.

"Do you have any questions for me?" Jason asked as he chewed his last bite. "It's a lot to take in. Werewolves are real, and there are a lot like me, mostly in Chicago."

"Werewolves!" Christina shook her head in bewilderment and asked Miranda, "You knew this? About him?"

"Yes. That's the real reason he couldn't stay for the party last night. It was the full moon."

Husband and wife exchanged glances, but both looked too stunned to ask anything. Jason decided to give them a quick introduction to werewolf basics.

"Okay, so I was created in a genetics lab. I wasn't bitten, cursed, or anything like that. I escaped from there three and a half years ago. Even though I established a good life in New York, there's always a chance they'll hunt me down and force me to go back."

"Right," Michael said sarcastically. "And it's okay for you to traipse around with our daughter and put her in danger?"

"Would you even care?" Miranda protested, rising from her seat as if to fight. Jason put his hand on her arm, and she sat back down, grumbling.

Michael drummed his fingertips on the table. "Say I believe you. How were you created in a lab? Were you a test tube baby or something?"

Miranda laughed without humor at the mention of test tube babies. Their missing embryos, courtesy of John Coleman, was source of mutual pain. Instead of focusing on that, Jason chose to answer Michael.

"In a roundabout way, yes. I was born human and kidnapped when I was fourteen. Gene therapy permanently changed me, and there is no reversal. I am a werewolf. I don't miss whatever being human was." He paused and muttered, "Besides, all the monsters I ever knew had human faces."

Christina and Michael were both silent as they mentally manipulated all the new information. While waiting, Jason got a glass of water and devoured another sandwich.

"Does it hurt?" Christina asked him in a small voice.

"Not anymore, thankfully." He wiped any last crumbs away from his mouth. "I will be doing it for the rest of my life. There is no such thing as werewolf menopause. My only rest is death."

"So... you both know about each other," Michael said, pointing fingers at both of them, "and you're okay with it?"

"Yeah," Miranda said eloquently.

With more enthusiasm, Jason said, "I can see the energy field that lives all around her. It moves and connects her to everything. Miranda saved the life of a woman who didn't even know she was in mortal danger!"

Jason knew he should probably feel embarrassed about gushing, but Miranda's parents were listening. Maybe they could learn through him how wonderful she was. "She shines so brightly sometimes, I can't see anything else but her. It's absolutely intoxicating."

Miranda had been staring up at the ceiling as if embarrassed by his words of praise. She became serious as she leaned forward on the table. "Mom, Dad, you can't tell anyone that Jason is a werewolf. The lab he ran away from is bad news. They might track him down and take me like a two-for-one special. It's already happened once."

"Excuse me?" Christina asked, turning her head as if to hear them better.

"Right after Thanksgiving, one of the geneticists from the project kidnapped both of us. He said my fire powers exemplified natural evolution, while Jason was all about forced evolution. Together, we made the perfect genetic cocktail to make perfect werewolf babies."

Jason was surprised she'd actually talked about it. Maybe it was the morning for all secrets to come to light. He squeezed Miranda's hand to offer comfort, but the other side of the table had a different story entirely. Christina looked horrified, and Michael stood up so quickly his chair toppled over.

Pointing in Jason's face, the older man shouted, "The hell you're making babies with my daughter! I'll cut it right off if you ever try to touch her again."

Christina said, "Like we've ever been able to control her sex life!"

"Shut! Up!" Miranda stood, clenching her fists. "Jason is my person, whether you like it or not. I just wanted you to know that someone kidnapped me and hurt me. And more than that, it wasn't the first time!"

She sighed and put her hands in her pockets. "I've been trying to remember everything that happened at the church that night, and... I still don't know how I got there. I should, but I don't."

Miranda's aura was cloudy with confusion. Jason hated seeing her like that. He got up and took her in his arms.

"Get me out of here," she whispered into his chest at a volume that only he could hear with his enhanced senses.

"So... we're done for now. I need to call New York, and Miranda needs to rest." Jason quickly cleaned up any evidence of their sandwich making. As he ushered Miranda out of the room, he attempted politeness by saying, "Thank you for an interesting morning."

CHAPTER EIGHT

Miranda's muddled dreams as she slept through most of that Christmas Eve morning returned repeatedly to the church and the inherent mystery of what had actually happened to her. A face she couldn't see danced through her memory. How had she gotten there? Was she stolen from her parents or her grandparents? She could ask her parents for details of that night, but it would have to wait until her mental fortifications were a little stronger.

She'd gone to sleep in Jason's arms, but when she woke, his side of the bed was cool to the touch. At the sound of children's laughter and the high peal of a Christmas carol played jauntily on the violin, there was no doubt of his whereabouts. The time, though? Miranda had no idea but guessed it to be afternoon.

No one was at her door demanding her presence, so she took a quick shower. She patted her long hair dry while selecting her Christmas Eve outfit, a pair of soft green jeans and a Cornell sweatshirt in the school colors of carnelian, gray, and white. She topped it off with a headband that had reindeer antlers on it. The only thing Miranda didn't add was a red Rudolph nose.

She retrieved a flat, wrapped package that had been hiding at the bottom of her luggage. It was something she'd picked up the previous weekend when having a fun night with Lisa. It was also the only present she'd gotten for anyone. Gift in hand, Miranda headed downstairs.

In the living room below, Christina sat on the loveseat with Abby and Molly in their matching dresses. Jackson sat on the floor with his cousins Riley and Oliver. They all had their eyes fixed on Jason, who stood by the Christmas tree with his violin tucked under his arm. He was in the middle of signing something to the children, but upon sight of Miranda, he smiled brightly at her.

The children were a very attentive audience. If the Pied Piper was a thing, could Jason be called the Fied Fiddler? It was, perhaps, a silly thought, but he really did have a knack with children.

Monty and Mitch were talking with Michael about farm equipment that Monty needed to repair at his place. Caroline hovered near her husband's side, a drink of Christmas cocoa in hand. Jessica was in the kitchen but came right out to speak to Miranda.

"Do you want to eat before we open up the presents?"

"No. Go ahead without me." She wasn't expecting to get anything this year after arriving on short notice. "I'll make myself a plate and watch everyone else."

Tucking the present away from view, Miranda dashed to the kitchen and put together a plate of cookies and finger sandwiches. What she really wanted was nachos. That could be a new Christmas tradition for her and Jason. They could style it with all the different colored tortilla chips.

"I see Sean let you use his car," Mitch said as she walked by.

"Yup." Miranda hid the wrapped package under her thigh as she sat on the fireplace stones. She could be a modern Cinderella instead of any other fairy tale princesses she'd been playing lately. "He's going to teach Jason to drive."

That was a bald-faced lie. It was easy to lie when she was saying absurd things. This was perhaps not a point of pride.

Dropping down beside her, Jason asked, "He is?"

Miranda shrugged and took a bite of cookie. "He might if we ask him nicely and pay for the gas."

"I was watching you drive last night. I have an idea how it works." He mimed many limbs moving, more like someone doing chair yoga than driving a classic American muscle car.

"I didn't think there was enough light to see what I was doing." Miranda nibbled at a tasty chicken salad sandwich. She'd have to compliment Caroline, who served them at open-house viewings.

"One of my silver-eyed gifts is being able to see in the dark." Jason tapped his temple. "Not that it matters. You're always the brightest spot in the room."

"The brightest... in the room?" Mitch asked with a cough. "What do you mean by that?"

"Oh. I can see her aura," Jason said. "None of the rest of you have one like hers, but maybe your grandchildren will."

"Oh, sure. Auras. Like I believe that hogwash," Jessica said with a scoffing laugh and a look to the others to agree with her.

Mitch, on the other hand, blanched. "You *told* him?"

"I didn't, actually," Miranda said, talking with her mouth full again. "He figured it out, and then I confirmed it when he guessed right."

"And it doesn't... scare you?" Mitch whispered to Jason.

"No. It intrigues me," he answered with a soft glance in her direction. "I feel like a moth to her flame."

It was a very sweet sentiment, but Miranda was more surprised by her brother. This was the first time in a long time that Mitch had acknowledged any awareness of Miranda's flame-powered soul. Her brothers as a unit acted ignorant of her special abilities, so much so she didn't expect any of her sisters-in-law to be aware of the dirty family secret.

Christina got up and kissed her husband's cheek as she walked by him, a small gesture of married normalcy that made Miranda think of Lurlene and Joel. Now that they knew more about Jason and what they'd been through together, could her parents be happy she'd found someone as different as herself? That hope was more optimistic than prudent.

Jason volunteered to hand out the presents to everyone. He joked that it would prove he knew everyone's names. The miracle of a mostly pleasant Christmas Eve after the last two days and that morning was wrinkling Miranda's brain. It was what she wanted, but it felt strange to get it.

"Oh." Jason stared at a wrapped item that was likely a mug with hot chocolate mix. "One for me and one for Miranda from Jessica, Monty, Riley, and Oliver."

Jessica scrunched her face. "Don't open those. Santa didn't realize you hated peppermint."

"There are a lot of people for Santa to think about, so maybe," he brought the two presents to Riley and Oliver, "you two can give these very nice gifts to Pops and Nan tomorrow."

The children giggled, and Monty nodded his head in approval.

Some of the biggest packages under the tree were for Mitch and Caroline's trio of children. They tore through the paper with glee to find toys and more boxes of things that needed assembling.

"You can do that with the kids the day after Christmas," Mitch said to his wife with a smirk.

"No, you can do it because I have a showing that day. Real estate never stops when you're as good as I am," Caroline said, brushing her knuckles on her shirt proudly.

"Trying to get your sales quota in before the end of the year?" asked Jessica with a salute of her beverage.

"I'll help!" Jason volunteered. "Miranda and I could probably put everything together. No problem. We're good at working together."

Mitch gave him the stink eye, something Miranda had temporary empathy with. He could have asked her first before obligating them to help. But maybe it would go toward smoothing things out between them.

"Yeah, okay. But you aren't allowed to do any... activities in my house or in front of my kids. I don't want that kind of nasty near them."

Jason put his hands up in surrender then sat down on the hearthstones beside Miranda.

In the quiet moment, she handed him the present she'd been hiding. "Merry Christmas."

His face went on an emotional journey before freezing in open-mouthed surprise.

"When did you get this?" He turned it over several times.

"Last weekend. Call it an impulse buy." When Jason didn't tear into the paper right away, she quipped, "Unless X-ray vision is one of your talents, you should open it up."

He got over his apparent case of shyness, and the ripped paper made a small rain of confetti around them. Inside the package was a drawing pad, pencils, a compass, a protractor, and several other tools for technical drawing. He was unnaturally still as he picked through everything. Miranda couldn't tell if he liked it or if the present was one of her bad ideas.

After a few seconds, Jason signed to her, [Thank you. This is amazing! How did you think of it?]

Miranda spoke because she wasn't fluent enough to explain using only Sign. "If you're going to be a luthier, I figured you might want to have something to make your technical drawings."

"It's perfect!" He lunged forward to give her a kiss she got lost in for a few seconds.

Once they pulled their mouths apart, Monty asked Jason, "Tell me again why you weren't at Pops's birthday party last night."

"I had things to do."

"Our sister," Mitch said under his breath.

Miranda sighed at the teasing. At least it was easier to take than the hostile reactions to her fire power.

"Hey, I want to ask you something," she said to her parents and brothers. "How did I get to the church when I was five years old. What exactly happened?"

Monty sat on the arm of the sofa like a bird on a limb. "What are you talking about? What church?"

"Do you mean the one where Pops burned his hand?" Mitch asked. "That happened in a church."

"Oh. I thought Pops got burned because he was a member of the volunteer fire department," Monty said. "I had early admission at U of M, so I wasn't here when it happened."

"Yes, that church!" Miranda said, throwing out her hands for emphasis. "How did I get there? Did someone steal me from you, or was I offered up like an Old Testament sacrifice?"

"What are you talking about?" Caroline asked, confusion marring her features.

"Not a clue," Jessica told her in commiseration.

Miranda stood up and paced her small area in front of the fireplace. "When I was five years old, someone kidnapped me and tried to drown me. Pops was there to save me, but he got hurt."

"Sure, Randy," Jessica said skeptically. "Why would anyone try to kidnap you?"

"Fear? There are things I can do that others can't. It's a secret we don't talk about, but it's still true."

"Like what?" Caroline asked.

"Yeah, what can you do, Auntie?" Jackson piped up.

She shook her head at her two sisters-in-law. This was going to be difficult. Maybe less so if she admitted something most of them had seen. "I lit the candles on Pops's cake."

"We know that," Jessica said, not impressed.

"Miranda, don't," Christina said.

"You don't! I'm not going to hide from my own family anymore!" Her voice sounded petulant even to her own ears.

Instead of speaking further, Miranda lifted her hands above her head as if weaving a spell, and she let colored sparkles shine around her like a mystical crown and rain down upon her. Then she brought her hands together, all the points of light coalescing into a single flame above her index finger. She snapped, and it disappeared.

Caroline and Jessica both had matching open-mouthed expressions, but the children clapped enthusiastically at her show.

"Again!" exclaimed Abby.

"Wow," Jackson said.

"It's so pretty," chimed in Riley.

[Thank you,] Miranda signed to them.

Riley eagerly signed back, [You're welcome.] It was a sweet move that made Miranda put her hand over her heart.

"Miranda can make fire do anything she wants," Jason said into the tender moment, "and it connects to her inner light. I'm sure there are others somewhere who can influence other types of energy, but neither of us has met anyone yet."

Exhibiting a practical mind, Monty asked, "How would you know if you did?"

"No clue," Miranda said.

Jason stroked his chin in a philosopher pose. "I assume I'd see their auras the same way I see Miranda's."

"Do any of you know anything about the church?" Miranda asked again, soul weary about something she should know. Then she confessed her maudlin self-doubt. "Sometimes I wonder if you all would have been happier if I died back then. Then I wouldn't be your problem sister or daughter."

Jason's face reflected his sadness for her, but the other adults in the room looked like they wanted to be anywhere but right where they were.

Breaking the silence, Christina said, "Oh, Malcolm," and turned away.

Michael whisper-shouted at his wife. "Christina! We're not supposed to talk about it!"

Miranda studied her parents and brothers once more. When had any of them stood up for her and how damaged she'd been? Her sense of unfairness and betrayal added vinegar to the already salted wound.

"I'm going to the barn."

Jason rose to go with her, but he had become surrounded by children during Miranda's probing questions. Despite the tension in the room with the adults, Riley had purposed herself to be his personal hairdresser and was putting microbraids in his bushy mop. Miranda shook her head for him to stay behind.

She put her shoes on at the back door and stepped outside. Right then, her internal fire burned too hot to need anything else.

AS MUCH AS JASON WANTED to be with Miranda, he understood the craving for solitude. That was one of the reasons he'd often sat on the roof outside his window in Ithaca. He found peace communing with the night. So, he remained in the living room while the other adults ignored him. Maybe that was a good thing given how much attention he'd gotten that morning about his lycanthropy.

Jessica and Caroline talked with their husbands to find out more about Miranda's power. For his own peace of mind, Jason ignored those conversations. After a few minutes, he tried to stand again, but Riley, who was still micro-braiding his hair, tumbled into his arms with a giggle. Then Oliver and Jackson jumped toward him, so Jason dropped back down on the floor. Abby regarded the whole thing as if she wasn't too sure about her cousins' shenanigans, but her twin Molly ran into the fray.

"Oh, sweet Mozart!" Jason said from the bottom of a pile of children.

He crawled out from underneath them, and Jason directed his attention to loading up different presents into the different family vehicles. It let him get some fresh air and see Miranda's aura glowing from a distance in the barn. Once he finished that self-appointed task, he entertained the children with more stories in American Sign Language until they were ready to go. Jessica and Caroline had other relatives in the area they needed to visit.

"Don't forget," he said to Mitch and Caroline as they were leaving, "Miranda and I can help put together all the toys the day after Christmas. We don't mind helping."

"We'll see," Mitch replied in a tone that made it seem not very likely.

Inside the house without their children around, Michael and Christina had the silent arguments of long-married couples. The glares were loud and cutting, but Jason didn't know what they meant. He packed his things and retreated to Miranda's girlhood bedroom.

Once he was alone, Jason admired all over again the thoughtful present Miranda had given him. It was so simple and perfect with thick paper, pencils, and different tools he might need to make his design concepts into realities.

Flexing his left hand a few times, Jason remembered one of his frequent experiences in the lab. The White Coats had broken his bones many times, especially the small ones in his hands and feet. They wanted to know about werewolf healing factors. Jason had recovered, but the potential loss of music had wounded him more than those experiments ever could.

With his brand-new Christmas present in hand, Jason had the inspiration to sketch an idea. He could take Pops's existing violin and modify it to be played left-handed. Maybe he could help Pops have music joy in his life again. Jason smiled at the paper with his first plans as a future luthier. This would work.

When he looked up, Miranda still wasn't back in the house. It was time to find her. If nothing else, she could send him away, but he could at least show her he cared.

Jason gathered a blanket and went downstairs to throw together an evening picnic. He felt odd digging in the fridge, but his hunger won out. Starvation had been part of his life so long that he still wasn't sure what being full was like. He settled on some apples, milk, and the makings for peanut butter and jelly sandwiches.

He slipped on a long-sleeved flannel shirt and a pair of shoes to walk out to the barn. It looked pristine, turned into something tidy by all Miranda's energy while she'd been hiding out. She was currently sitting on a stool in the middle lane of the barn with her back against the door to one of the horse stalls.

"Are you ready for company yet?"

She looked up and gave him an empty stare. He put the basket down beside her, showing his humble offering of food.

Leaning over to pick through the offerings, Miranda said, "I'm surprised you didn't bring your marshmallows and sausages."

"If that's what you want, I'll go back and get them, but I was hoping to save that for something fun, like New Year's Eve."

Miranda picked an apple, turned it over to take off the produce sticker, and rubbed it on her sweatshirt before taking a bite. She chewed without engaging in conversation, but the horse nickered at her. Miranda gave it the rest of her apple while Jason made her a sandwich. He also propped the milk between them.

She took that too, and the more Miranda ate, the more solid she became. It was as if she'd left her body and had only now decided to return. Jason often had fanciful thoughts like that but felt silly mentioning them out loud.

"I remember how I got to the church." Miranda's voice didn't have anger or the numbness of shock. It was merely a declaration of fact. "Everything started because I liked horses. When I came out here and started taking care of them, I remembered."

She reached for the quart of milk and wiped her face with the back of her wrist after she'd taken a long swig.

"What do you need me to do?" Jason could listen or ask questions. He could be quiet. Whatever she needed him to do, he'd do it.

"If I have a nightmare tonight, hold me." She held eye contact while he answered.

"Done. Gladly."

Miranda nodded. "Tomorrow is not going to be an easy day. I'm going to confront him."

Jason had an idea about who the most likely *him* was, but until Miranda showed her hand, he wouldn't know for sure.

A shift in her attention suddenly put her full scrutiny on him. "How are *you*? My parents aren't exactly thrilled about you being a werewolf."

He clenched his jaw, a mirthless mockery of a smile. "I'm not ashamed of who I am, but there's a burden in being known. Your parents hold my safety in their hands."

Miranda leaned back to the stall door, her fingers intertwined over her belly. After a minute or so of silence, she declared, "If I ever have children, I'm never treating them like this."

"No. We'll make our own mistakes."

She gave him a quizzical look then settled back to her tired calm. "I supposed we will."

They stayed in the barn a while longer, and Jason ended up falling asleep beside her. Certainly not the worst place he'd ever slept when he'd been on the run from the lab. Miranda woke him after midnight, when it was technically Christmas Day. They packed everything back to the house, and Jason wondered what kind of excitement the daylight would bring.

CHAPTER NINE

The steering wheel of Sean's GTO was innocent. Truly. But Miranda couldn't help strangling it as she prepared for the Christmas Day dinner at her grandparents' place. She was armored for potential battle in slim-fit jeans, a multi-colored asymmetrical tunic on top, and brown snow boots with tassels. Her hair was loose down her back but held away from her face with clear combs. She felt cute, and Miranda needed that confidence.

"Do you understand the timing between the clutch and the gas?" she asked Jason, who had requested a more explicit driving demonstration.

"I think so. It reminds me of playing the organ," he said.

Sometimes her boyfriend was really odd for reasons that had nothing to do with being a werewolf. The comment helped Miranda get out of her own head. "I thought you'd say drummer."

"Nope. An organist uses their feet more than a drummer does. They even have special shoes!" He looked rather pleased to know that fact.

"Oh, Lord," she groaned as she started the car. "I have got to teach you more about horses so we have an equal relationship."

Jason stroked his chin. "Can we ride horses to your grandparents' house from here? It isn't very far, is it?"

"We could," Miranda allowed. "In an emergency, it's straight through the woods, but I still have to bring Sean his car. So, let's drive."

Jason leaned over, his head almost resting on her shoulder as she started the car and shifted into reverse.

"You still have little braids in your hair," Miranda pointed out.

He sighed. "Riley."

"I can't fault the girl for taking a shine to you. I like you a little bit."

His silver eyes lifted to hers, amusement dancing in their depths. The tingle in her belly reminded Miranda that they hadn't been together so long that she was immune to his charms. Jason had always been charming, even when she'd been in firm denial about wanting him.

She drove the circuitous route to her grandparents' house while Jason grumbled about cutting the braids out and waiting until the next full moon for his hair to grow back in. Then he threw her for a loop with another off-the-wall, yet totally werewolf comment.

"I can't wait to put a face to Sean's scent."

"Uh..." Flummoxed would be the word to describe what she felt right then.

"I could find him in a crowd. His scent is all over this car. I just don't know which specific Lennox features he'll have."

Miranda downshifted as they neared the driveway to Pops and Nan's house. "Red hair and good looks, just like the rest of us."

She added a cheesy grin and parked as far away from the door as she could get. At least Sean would be able to go as he pleased instead of being hemmed in by other family members who arrived later.

When they got out, Jason hiked the strap of his violin case over his shoulder. He was fully prepared if there was a sudden need for Christmas carols or an impromptu musical duel with the devil.

Unless entertainment like that only happened in Georgia. Miranda wasn't entirely sure.

Pops and Nan had a single-story house that fit the sprawling ranch aesthetic. Behind the house was a barn that had horses and equipment. The place was already full of uncles, aunts, and cousins. It was also loud enough that she eyed Jason to see if his sensitive ears were bothered. He sniffed the air several times.

"Sean's here," the werewolf declared.

"Oh, yeah? Prove it. Take me to him."

Jason chuffed a laugh and confidently walked ahead of her to a group of adults in their twenties. Without error he stopped right in front of Sean, who was gesticulating with an unlit cigarette in his hand and generally being the life of the party.

"Sean?" Jason asked politely.

The other man turned toward him and looked Jason up and down. "So you're the guy who was schtupping my cousin in the closet."

"Schtupping?" Jason asked. "How do you know Yiddish?"

"The same way I do," Miranda said as she hooked her arm in Jason's.

"Mel Brooks movies," she and Sean chorused together.

Lifting his hand almost like a Catholic blessing, Sean said, "May the Schwartz be with you." Then, angling closer to Miranda, he said, "Gimme a light."

Miranda rolled her eyes indulgently but granted his wish. She touched her fingertip to the end of the cigarette, something she felt added to the drama, and watched it blaze to life. Sean winked at her as he took a drag.

Dangling the key fob in the air, she said, "I owe you big time for letting me use your car, but we have another favor to ask."

"What's that?" Sean pocketed the keys in a swift motion.

"Jason doesn't know how to drive yet." She put her free hand on his chest as if his identity was in doubt. "Think you could teach him?"

"Probably. Why don't you drive?"

"I grew up in a big city with reliable public transportation and didn't need to know."

Sean flicked his ashes. "Well, out here, you do. We could do a little driving before we eat. It's going to take a while to get everything ready."

Miranda left the two men to get to know each other and picked her way across the yard, like a boxer ready to go into the ring. She wasn't sure what round she was on, but it was time to go up against her opponent on equal footing.

As she was approaching, Riley bolted out the door. She fully expected the girl to run past her to Jason since he had easily won the children's hearts. Her niece surprised her by jumping into her arms instead.

"Pretty auntie." Riley slipped her arm around Miranda's neck. "Let me braid your hair."

"Not right now. I need to talk to Pops." With a hug, she set her niece back down. "We'll do it later, okay?"

Miranda had to focus on her mission before she lost her courage.

Once inside the house, she headed to the kitchen where Nan and a few of the family women were chatting. Pops wasn't there, and Nan explained that he, Uncle Ronald, and a few of the other men were trying to deep fry a turkey behind the house.

Miranda facepalmed. That was one of the most dangerous modes of cooking if done improperly. She was the supposed firebug, yet the family around her did plenty of stupid fire-related tricks.

"Did you get sick Sunday night?" Nan asked. "You left the birthday party so soon after the cake."

"Neither Dad nor Pops liked the way I lit the candles." Changing subjects, Miranda asked, "Do you remember how I got to the church when I was a little girl? The one where Pops burned his hand?"

"Well, I don't know," Nan said before sampling some broth from one of the pots. "It was so long ago."

"Fourteen years in February," Miranda said. "You surely remember when your husband left with a hand that worked and came back with one that didn't."

Nan clicked the spoon on the side of the pot but didn't look at her.

Using a different tactic, Miranda asked, "Was Pops *really* a volunteer firefighter? Everyone says he was, but I don't remember it. I didn't meet any of his old fire crew while I was still at the party."

"He was," Nan confirmed with a nod. "For a few months a lot of fires started cropping up around the area, and we needed the volunteers. He was in training with the local fire department. After his injury, he didn't continue with it."

The other women in the kitchen filed out as Nan gave them a look. Not wasting the private moment, Miranda pounced on her grandmother's knowledge.

"What else do you know about the night the church burned?"

The noise of family chatter in the rest of the house overpowered the sound of sauces bubbling in their pots while Nan considered her answer.

"You were here, and then you weren't. I thought you went with Malcolm to investigate the fire. You were always at his side when you were a little girl. He called you his Clara."

Scrunching her face, Miranda remembered him doing that. She hadn't thought it odd at the time because Clara was so close to Claire. She always thought Pops was being playful, but what if he wasn't? Did it mean anything?

As if reading her thoughts, Nan said, "Clara Ferguson was your grandfather's girlfriend. She died in Scotland before Malcolm and I met on the boat. I didn't know he still had a photo of her until Caroline put it in the collage for his birthday."

Nan checked the bread in the oven and stirred the pots on the stove. "I'm an old woman. Clara's ghost doesn't haunt me, but I think it still haunts Malcolm."

Miranda, still very much alive and not a ghost, blew out a breath of frustration. "That wasn't very helpful, Nan."

The older woman leveled her a look as if she had just been trying to impart some wisdom that wasn't received. After her own sigh, Nan said, "You should talk to your grandfather. He might open up to you. I have a feeling you two need to clear the air."

"If he'll even talk to me. He told me not to come."

Miranda exited the house to find the men out back. Just as she did that, Sean and Jason got in the GTO and sped away. Or as speedily as they could go with Jason grinding the gears. She laughed because he would be so annoyed with himself until he got it right. But that was Sean's problem right now.

She rounded the corner of the house to find her dad, Pops, Uncle Ronald, and a few others gathered around a huge stainless steel pot. In the time-honored tradition of men cooking outside, several of them had longneck beers. Pops was telling everyone about a Christmas mishap involving one of her uncles and a bull from a neighbor's pasture. It was entertaining the first few times she'd heard it, but it was an often-told story by this point.

"Pops, can we talk?" Miranda asked when the old man took a breath.

Though he'd been jovial and entertaining just a moment before, a storm cloud passed over his face at the sight of her. He quickly plastered on a smile as if it had been an inconsequential microexpression.

"What do you need, Miranda, lass?"

"Alone, please." She glanced at her father, whose face she could not read, and the uncles who surrounded them.

"I can't leave this turkey," Pops said. "Can it wait until later?"

It was a nice deflection, but Uncle Ronald spoke up. "I've got this, Dad. You and Miranda go talk."

"Thanks," she told her uncle. To Pops, she said, "Let's go talk in the barn."

She took Pops by the left elbow, smiling softly to give the impression of being a sweet granddaughter. It wasn't at all that she was marching him into the barn where so many of her early problems had started.

When they arrived in the darkened building, he shook her off. "I don't appreciate you manhandling me! I told you, you aren't welcome here!"

"Right, well. I don't imagine you're going to appreciate anything I'm about to do. I want the truth, Pops."

"About what?" he asked, his lip curling in disgust.

"For a very long time," she started, hands clasped in front of her, "I didn't remember how I got to the church. It was like my brain locked all the dark memories away to protect me. But I knew you came to rescue me. I loved you, and you were my hero."

Pops shifted his weight from side to side. "I don't hear a question yet."

"I'm getting there," she snapped. "Last night, I finally remembered. *You* took me to the church. *You* handed me over to those people."

Miranda pointed outside as if a mob of peasants was waiting for her with pitchforks and torches. "All these years, I thought I'd been kidnapped, but I wasn't! You handed me over like a sacrifice."

An oily smile spread over Pops's face as his spine uncoiled. "How else was I going to get the fire demon out of you?"

She gasped, recoiling as if she'd been struck. Did he really think that? With exacting stillness, Miranda stared down her grandfather. "How could you do that?"

Under her calm exterior, her stomach roiled. The truth couldn't be worse than what her mind had made up for the last fourteen years. Malcolm Lennox, on the other hand, was tight-lipped and refused to look at her.

Miranda clenched her fists. "Answer me!"

"Clara," he said with a scratchy voice, "you should never have followed me here."

"I'm not Clara." It took everything to hold back screams of uncontrollable rage. "Who do you think I am? The ghost of your dead girlfriend?"

She had spoken in absurdity because everything about the situation was absurd. Pops turned completely pale and slowly edged away from her.

"Is... is that what you think?" Miranda asked.

"Of course it's you!" He could only spare a lightning-fast glance before looking anywhere in the barn but at her. "I left you in Scotland, Clara! You cheating whore. I came to America to get away from you, but you couldn't leave me be."

"Do you even hear yourself? I'm Miranda, not Clara!" Was Pops battling dementia?

"I killed you," he said, with a gaze like surgical steel, "but you waited until I was comfortable in a good life to haunt me."

Fear gripped her, sending cold waves up and down her spine. So Pops killed Clara and thought Miranda was… what? Her reincarnation or possessed by the woman's ghost? But if he had killed her…

Quietly, lest she spook him, Miranda asked, "How did you do it?"

Pops waved his damaged hand. "I burned you and your lover. You were supposed to be faithful to *me*! I did what I had to do. Everything was locked up neatly in the past until you showed up to claim vengeance."

Miranda had so many questions. Playing along with his delusion, she asked, "But how did you know I was secretly Clara?"

"Because only you could haunt me with the fire that killed you. I knew. I had to crush you before you got too strong."

Oh, life had certainly done its fair share of trying to crush her.

Continuing, Pops said, "I knew you were Clara as soon as Michael named you. You made sparks at me the first time you saw me as a child! There could be no doubt."

Yes, Miranda had made sparks as an infant. Any energy shifter child would surely manifest powers in times of joy. What had been an act of guileless love for her fueled the old man's paranoia. Then her parents sided with him to crush every fire-based expression of love she had.

Circling back to the original question, Miranda asked, "Why did you take me to the church?"

Pops practically vibrated with the righteousness of his conviction. "You had to be set free, Clara, to go back to the hell where you belonged."

Miranda closed her eyes against the memories of hands holding her struggling body down as if to drown her. Perhaps she'd been right all along. If she'd died in the water, then her grandfather would have been happy. Instead, he went off the rails and took her parents with him.

"Did my parents hate me so much that they would let you destroy me?"

He held his head up, the appearance of pride. "I made Michael fear the monster you were. Eventually, he saw I was right. There would be no victory for your hellfire. Anything of Clara that remained in you would be ground down again and again."

Miranda clutched at her chest because it hurt to breathe.

"My father agreed to that?" Learning that Michael had been guilted by his own father didn't make the knowledge pill easy to swallow. All this madness was caused by one man's guilty conscience.

So many thoughts wanted to intrude, but the loudest one was this. Pops had chosen fire as his weapon. Why that instead of a gun or some other means?

"Are you a fire shifter like me?" Miranda asked. Maybe her power had come from somewhere specific. Like a pyromaniac murderer of a grandfather.

"Is that what you call it?" His tone was a cruel acid. "I could never be like you."

"It doesn't mean you're not."

Miranda couldn't trust him to tell her the truth, but there was one person currently in the middle of a driving lesson who could.

She kept Pops in her sights while she called Sean. "You and Jason get back here immediately. I'm in the barn with Pops and need to ask him a question."

"Yeah, of course," Sean replied. "We're coming back right now anyway. Is something wrong?"

"Tell you about it when you get here." She ended the call without listening to his response.

"I'm not staying here with you, Clara. I've told you everything I'm going to say."

Miranda barely resisted the urge to scream at him. "You're not going anywhere!"

A clatter of feet outside the barn mere seconds later announced Sean and Jason's arrival. Sean threw open the door, and Jason's silver eyes flashed with panic as he looked for Miranda.

Thankful for Sign Language, Miranda asked, [Is Pops an energy shifter?]

Jason's eyebrows crinkled in confusion. He assessed the old man with only a glance. [No. Not at all. His aura has no elemental light.]

So much for that theory. Pops was merely human, and a rather damaged one at that. Miranda was back to being what she'd always been. Singular. Alone.

"Who is this?" Pops called out.

"Hi, Mr. Lennox! My name is Ja–"

"No!" she shouted across the barn. "You're not for him. Nothing I love belongs to *him*."

With soul-deep resignation, Miranda addressed her grandfather one last time. "I'm done with you."

Pops had kidnapped her, and all the fear and abuse in her life had come from his actions. He'd held her parents under his influence, and then it had fallen to her brothers like dominoes.

The old man's past sins were too much to unpack. Could she do anything about a murder from long before she or her father were born? Miranda didn't have the bandwidth right now to process it. So, she marched her boyfriend and cousin out of the barn, leaving Pops behind them.

Miranda blinked up at the winter sun, and for the first time in her nineteen years, she felt cold. Jason wrapped his arms around her, and though she appreciated his love beyond words, she would not let herself fall apart in front of witnesses. Her pride might not be worth much, but that and spite would be her shield until she figured out what to do next.

CHAPTER TEN

Hanging the strap to his violin case on the chair back at the card table where he and Miranda sat, Jason lamented that he probably wasn't going to use the instrument with Pops after all. He distracted himself with the food on his plate that was plentiful and stacked embarrassingly high. His werewolf metabolism meant he usually ate a lot when he did get the privilege of eating. Regular meals after he escaped the lab were a luxury he'd returned to only after the Rosens took him in. He could not freely enjoy the flavors of Christmas dinner, however, because he was more concerned about Miranda and whatever had happened between her and Pops.

She had clearly wanted to leave after confronting him in the barn, but they both got swept up in the wave of everyone going into the house to eat. Now at the table beside him, Miranda sat with her own plate, mentally checked out to somewhere Jason couldn't fathom. The table wasn't all silent, though. Sean sat with them and kept the light banter going. A woman wearing cheetah print with red accents joined them.

Sean made quick introductions. "Jason, this is my sister, Sheena. Our parents are Ronald and Nancy over there. Dad helped cook the turkey."

"Yeah, I'd heard about Uncle Ronald. Good turkey," he replied to Sean. "And I saw you, Sheena, setting up the photography station for the party."

"Oh, that's right! I saw you, too, before the party started. Why'd you leave?" She spread a cloth napkin across her lap after she sat down.

"Preexisting appointment I couldn't avoid."

Sheena's eyes showed she wasn't satisfied with his answer but was too polite to push for more information. She turned her attention to Miranda. "You did so well with the lights on the birthday cake. I don't know how you pulled it off!"

"Street magic," she said, stabbing her mashed potatoes as if they had offended her.

Jason put his hand on Miranda's shoulder to give her a loving touch. Instead of leaning into him, she removed his hand and held it down by their thighs. Sheena stared at the two of them as she chewed and then shot Sean a look as if to silently communicate her opinion.

"You don't look so good, Miranda," Sheena said.

"I'm dealing with a lot." A fine understatement if Jason ever heard one.

Sean must have seen the need for levity. He pointed at Jason's plate. "You're eating like a linebacker, but you don't have the body of one."

Sheena gave her brother's arm a backhanded slap and whispered, "Don't comment on someone else's eating habits. He could have an eating disorder. You don't know! Men get them, too."

Jason twirled the end of the fork between his fingers. "I don't have an eating disorder, just a very fast metabolism."

"I wish I had a fast metabolism like that," Sheena declared.

Miranda popped off with an unhinged laugh that made both Sean and Sheena jump. "Then she'd be a leopard shifter! Do you think those exist?"

[Maybe,] Jason signed.

The genetics lab that made him and the other werewolves probably could make any kind of shifter they wanted, including leopard shifters. All it would take was enough money and an army of researchers. And another army's worth of test subjects. Having been an involuntary test subject, Jason already knew that wasn't a very pleasant possibility.

When Malcolm Lennox walked through the room, Miranda's aura churned with bright sparks among the dull, dark red field. They danced around her like lightning bugs that wanted to fly to the old man. Before they could go, Miranda pulled them back and consolidated them within herself.

Sean also looked at his grandfather and back to Miranda. He leaned toward her. "What were you and Pops talking about in the barn? You look ready to kill him."

"Murder, arson, and superstitious delusions," she barked. "He's a fan."

"You're not acting like you were discussing his favorite kinds of books," Sheena said before delicately sipping through her recycled straw.

"I wasn't. Real crimes." Miranda's demeanor and aura changed to something much brighter as she sat up. "Sheen, you said you could make murder boards. How good are you at internet research?"

"The best," she said confidently. "Whatcha need?"

"Then you can help me find some answers. I need to learn everything you can find about Pops's old girlfriend, Clara Ferguson, starting with her obituary."

Though Jason appreciated Miranda being more animated, something was afoot. [Do you mean the woman from the photo?]

[Yes,] she signed, though her eyes were still on Sheena.

"When do you want to do that?" Sheena asked, worry making a valley in the middle of her forehead.

"As soon as possible. Now, even." Miranda pushed her chair back and stood. "I need to get out of here."

"Oh, okay." Sheena threw down her napkin to join her.

Jason tugged on Miranda's sleeve and hissed, "Not to be *that* werewolf, but I'm not done eating!"

He felt like a glutton as he pointed out the obvious, but he needed the calories.

"Bruh!" Sean laughed. "Did I just hear you call yourself a werewolf?"

"I didn't think you could hear that," Jason grumbled. So he wasn't the only one with great hearing at their table.

"I did, and you have some 'splaining to do, Lucy." Sean reached for Jason's plate. "I'll put this in a dish for you to take along. Then I'm going with you. This feels like an adventure I don't want to miss."

After Sean and Sheena left the table, Jason turned to Miranda, lightly caressing the outside of her forearms with his fingertips. He didn't know what questions to ask, but he was certain this wasn't the place to unload their hearts. So he went for the simple.

"I'm with you. Whatever you need."

"I know." Miranda looked up at him, softness showing in her brown eyes. "I don't know what I'm going to do yet, but I need to get the facts straight."

Jason slipped the strap of his violin case over his shoulder. Then they walked toward the door to gather their boots and coats. Miranda put her arm around his waist and reached into his hip pocket. It was a slick move.

Before they could leave, Aileen Lennox cornered Miranda and put her trembling hands on the younger woman's face.

"Did Malcolm tell you about Clara?"

"Yes." The odor of brimstone around Miranda increased, a peculiar reaction, though not the first time she'd done it. "How long have you known?"

"Suspicions for a long time, but I only found out for sure after the birthday party. Clara's photo in the collage was a tipping point for Malcolm."

Miranda stepped closer, an affectation of privacy, though Jason could have heard her from anywhere in the house. "What exactly did you learn?"

Nan wrung her hands and avoided her granddaughter's gaze. "He says it was an accident. That he was trying to scare the boyfriend. That's why I thought you could talk it out. Get the story directly, instead of second-hand."

"What was the boyfriend's name? Did he tell you?"

Glancing first to see if others were listening, Nan said, "Iain Craig."

"Thank you. That might be useful," Miranda said. "I love you, Nan, but I can't forgive him. I'm not coming back."

The finality in her voice implied the decision was for good, not just that day. Miranda hugged her grandmother and stepped out the front door. Jason waved to the woman he'd seen only one other time and followed his girlfriend out.

Sean waited for them with a smile and Jason's leftovers by his car. Instead of fighting with his lighter again, he held out his cigarette. "Please?"

And as easy as that, Miranda set it on fire. Then she asked the question Jason was thinking. "Where's Sheena?"

Pointing with the fingers that held the cigarette, Sean indicated where Sheena drove up to them in her stylish small SUV.

"An automatic like that would be easier for you to drive," Sean told Jason with an elbow bump.

"That sounds like a challenge," he replied, taking the leftovers.

Sean nodded and blew a smoke ring. Then he asked his cousin, "So what's Sheena going to do for you on the internet?"

"Research. Learn everything about Clara Ferguson or Iain Craig short of hiring a detective. Maybe there'll be something old newspapers online."

"You mean like a cold case?" Sean planted his hands on his hips and bugged his eyes at her. "Sheen eats that up! Murder podcasts, too."

"Exactly. Perfect person to help me," Miranda said.

Sheena slowed down enough for Miranda to get into the SUV, and without waiting for either of the men, they sped off. Jason blinked in surprise at the place where the license plate used to be.

"Okay..." Christmas Day was turning out to be a weird one.

Sean took the leftovers back like he and Jason had been playing a game of keep-away with it. "I'm feeling generous. You should drive again."

Jason raised his eyebrow. "Generous? Your cigarette's not done."

"That, too," Sean said, touching a new cigarette to the glowing ember of his old one. "Let's go."

Taking the driver's side, Jason secured his violin first. Then he buckled himself in and waited for Sean to teach him some more.

"You any good at that?" Sean asked, pointing to the violin case in the back seat.

"I'm okay. I'll play for you later if you want."

"Cool. Now don't forget the clutch..."

———⊙———

AS SHEENA SEARCHED the internet with her laptop, Miranda stared at her phone screen. She was tempted to call Joel Rosen and ask if they could come back to Ithaca early. Running away time and again wasn't practical, though. If she wanted a full separation from her parents and siblings, she would have to work at it methodically, starting with storage or disposal of her personal effects.

Sheena's apartment was maximalist in styling with walls full of pictures and fake plants growing out of places no real plant would find. She'd made a jungle of her home, living up to her comic book namesake.

It was roughly an hour later that Sean and Jason were at the door. Miranda opened it so as not to disturb Sheena's research.

"It doesn't take that long to drive here," she told them. "Were you grinding gears?"

"I was practicing," Jason said, which wasn't a denial.

Sean went into the other room to rubberneck his sister's research efforts. Meanwhile, Miranda heated Jason's leftovers in Sheena's microwave. Signing his thanks for finally getting his meal, he ate at the little kitchen table like food was going out of style. He might have even tasted it on the way down.

[What's on your mind?] Jason asked once the food was gone and his hands were free.

"Thinking about the best way to cut ties with my family," Miranda said. "I had to come back to find out for sure, but minimal contact is probably best. Except... I think we can help put together those toys for the kids."

He gave her a knowing look. "Because it's your nature to help, even if other people don't appreciate you."

She nibbled her fingernail and shrugged. "I'd like to think so."

Miranda glanced at Riley's little braids bobbing in his hair. They made her chuckle. Her nieces and nephews were all good kids. She wanted them to know her so they could make their own opinions about her. No matter how traumatized she was about her own reproductive options, she would be the best auntie they ever had.

In the other room, Sheena sent up a shout. Before Miranda could go see what she'd found, Sheena ran into the kitchen with her laptop in her hands. Sean was at her shoulder staring at what she had on the screen.

"I found her! I've got an article about Clara's death and her obituary. I. Am. Amazing!"

Sheena swung her hips and did a happy dance in place, all without letting go of her laptop. It was fun, but Miranda made grabby hands so she could read what her cousin had found.

The article about Clara's death indicated that she had been found in a burned-out industrial building with a man believed to be Iain Craig. Though it was believed to be arson, no suspects had been found. Her later obituary told of a life that had barely begun. Clara had been twenty when she died, only a few months older than Miranda was currently. Nothing there mentioned any ties, romantic or otherwise, to either Malcolm Lennox or Iain Craig. It was a short life, unfulfilled.

Miranda pushed the laptop back to her cousin. "Thank you, Sheena."

"So what now?" she asked.

"I don't know," Miranda said, clasping her hands together on the table, "but I should probably tell you that I can start fires with my brain. I don't know why, but I can. Pops is the one who committed the arson that killed Clara and Iain. That's what he told me in the barn. I just needed to find out if he was telling me the truth. My whole life, I thought he loved me, but he hated me because he thought I was the reincarnation of his dead girlfriend. If she even was his girlfriend. There's nothing here about him."

"Shit," Sean said. "That's messed up."

"To put it mildly," Miranda agreed.

Sheena's face was scrunched up, and she flicked her fingers as if she were trying to figure something out. "Wait. Is that how you were able to do everything with the candles?"

Miranda let out a startled laugh. "Yeah, it was!"

"Oh." Sheena took her hand. "You've always got us if you need anything."

"I wish I had known that when I was younger," Miranda replied with a gentle finger squeeze. "I would have been a lot less miserable."

"We're all damaged somehow, and none of us gets out of this one alive," Sean said in philosophical tones.

Sheena elbowed her brother. "Do you have something besides tobacco in that cigarette?"

He rolled his eyes and slid the cigarette back into his pocket. "So now that we've learned our grandfather is off his rocker, let's go do some family bonding. There's a pretty big storm rolling in tomorrow, so let's do something fun while we still can. I'm thinking we go blow shit up at the junkyard. Who's in?"

Miranda raised her hand. Sure, she had a lot of work ahead to set her life to rights on her own terms. It was still Christmas Day, though, and both Sean and Sheena had been supportive without fear and judgment. She would take the wins wherever she got them.

CHAPTER ELEVEN

On Wednesday evening, the day after Christmas, Miranda was exhausted. She and Jason had been at Mitch and Caroline's all day assembling toys to use inside and equipment for outside. Sure, they made a good team doing work that wasn't any harder than mucking a horse stall. There was just so much of it! Still, Miranda was proud of herself for helping her brother, and Mitch begrudgingly appreciated it.

Sheena called Miranda several times during the day and admitted she'd fallen down a research hole. Then she promised to tell a huge story once Miranda was done with toy assembly duty. She might look forward to Sheena's findings once she got over being so ungodly tired.

Being around three children under the age of six for a full day reinforced Miranda's firm belief that she was not ready to have any children of her own. It was better than any contraception available on the market. The children had probably been energized by the storm Sean had predicted. It rolled in as she and Jason returned to her parents' house.

She fell into her nest of blankets and pillows ready to sleep until the New Year, which could be a very real possibility. Jason curled up beside her, just as worn out as she was. His breath was already heavy and steady. She closed her eyes and followed him into dreamland.

In the depth of Miranda's mental fog, she heard something pounding. She decided to ignore it so it would go away. Sleep was more important. The sound stopped, only to be followed by a hand on her arm, shaking her awake.

She let out a yelp and looked up into her father's worried face. He was so close, she could count his pores. Michael looked utterly spooked.

"It's Pops and Nan," he panted. "Their house is on fire!"

Miranda's brain was still wandering in the fog, so she didn't immediately think of her own ability to tame fire. "Did you call the fire department?"

"Of course I did! The storm is blocking all travel in and out of their road. The emergency vehicles won't get there in time."

He sat in front of her, curling his body in on itself. Not once had Miranda ever remembered her father crying, but his eyes were suspiciously shiny. Behind her, Jason sat rigid against her back.

"You've got to save your grandparents!" Her father grabbed her hand. "You said you could put out fires. So do it!"

Miranda's built-up anger loosened her tongue. "Sure. Now that there's a threat to someone you *actually* care about, then what I can do is okay."

"We don't have time for arguments and apologies. You can't let them die!" Tears really did well in the corners of Michael's eyes that time. "You're the only one who can help."

"Pops doesn't deserve my help," she said, low and deadly like an animal about to strike.

Jason stood and tossed a few items into a drawstring bag. Quietly, he said, "Maybe he doesn't. But *you* do."

"What are you talking about?" Miranda demanded with a sneer in Jason's direction. She was ready to throttle him, but he looked unaffected by her ire as he packed.

"Don't let him compromise who you are, the person I know and love." Jason put his hand over his heart, again showing "I love you" fingers. "You would help a stranger in need. Now the people who need you are strangers with familiar faces."

Oh, that was low. Miranda hated that Jason made perfect sense. Her family might never appreciate her. But *she* would know she'd done the right thing. And so would Jason.

"I guess we're doing this."

Miranda threw off her blanket and scrambled for a change of clothing. Her father jumped to his feet but got out of her way. Though the main roads were blocked, she and Jason could take the path through the woods that connected the two properties.

"Is the snowmobile gassed up?" she asked her dad.

Michael's face fell. So much for that idea.

"Then go saddle a horse." Miranda sighed as she thought of running through the woods in a blizzard.

"Two of them?" Michael swept his gaze to include Jason.

"Just one. I don't know how to ride yet," the werewolf said as he stripped out of his clothing. "I'll be going on four legs."

"Are you sure?" The question was a little silly given Jason's state of undress.

"Of course! Which is why I've packed a bag." He tightened the straps around his shoulders, looking like a nudist hiker in the process. "I'm not going to freeze my tail off when the excitement is over."

Without further words, Jason shifted into a wolf that dominated the room. Though he had been quick, the shift was so noisy that Miranda wanted to retch in sympathy.

"I'm still not used to that," she whispered to her father. "Now, go! Saddle the horse."

He looked as pale as Miranda felt, but Michael raced ahead to do what she'd asked.

She and Jason went downstairs to the kitchen where Miranda guzzled a bottle of electrolyte water to fortify her for whatever battle they were facing.

"Miranda," Christina said, leaning against the kitchen wall with her hand on her chest. "He's got Riley."

She couldn't quite wrap her head around it. "Okay, okay... where are they? And who's all there? Tell me what you know!"

"Sheena called. Nan's shoulder might be broken. No idea where in the house they are."

"Nan, Sheena, and Riley," Miranda muttered. "Others?"

"I don't know," Christina sobbed.

Closing her eyes to find strength, Miranda reached out to her side to touch the werewolf. He was under her fingers in an instant. Was this going to be a twisted recreation of the church? No one was going to die this time if Miranda could help it. But it was time to act.

"I'll do what I can, Mom."

Jogging to the door, Miranda put on her layers of clothes. It didn't matter that she could control fire. A Montana blizzard was no joke. She could still get frostbite and so much more damage.

Outside the snow twinkled in the light, but it blew so heavily that the barn was barely visible. She trusted herself to find it only because she'd routinely walked between the buildings for so many years. Snow bit at the few exposed parts of her face.

Miranda stepped into the barn with Jason beside her. Michael held the horse's reins out. He nervously darted glances at Jason but didn't speak. Before taking the reins, Miranda snatched a pair of riding goggles often used with the snowmobile. Then she moved to the horse to double-check the cinch and the rest of the gear. She wouldn't be able to save anyone if she was thrown because of faulty tack.

As she worked, Miranda sent her warmth into the horse to gently calm him. *Everything is fine. I'll take care of you.* It took only a few seconds for the horse to settle. Satisfied, she put her foot in the stirrup and swung herself up into the saddle.

"Call emergency services and get someone there. We won't know if we need an ambulance until we get there."

"I will. Good luck." Michael clutched at her hand but then let it go so she could ride.

Calling down to Jason, Miranda said, "Follow me. There's a regular path we can use that shouldn't be too dangerous."

With that, she raced out of the barn toward the woods. The gibbous moon was hidden behind the clouds, and Miranda hadn't thought to include a headlight. They'd have to get by without it.

Her head low over the horse's neck and shoulders, Miranda kept her eyes trained on the path to make sure she could see anything that might injure the horse. The wind blew against them, stabbing them with cold and trying to work its way under her clothes. Though she craved speed and haste, it was slow going through the woods. A massive fire could have already done its damage by now.

Miranda cast her senses out ahead of her. Maybe her internal fire could reach ahead to the fire that burned at her grandparents' house. Nothing. They weren't close enough yet. She encouraged the horse to keep going with words of praise he might not be able to hear and reassuring pats to his neck.

At last, after too many minutes traveling through the woods, they surged across the thick and snowy tree line to enter her grandparents' property. The fire blazed over the house, a cacophony of color and sound, with a trail of fire leading to the barn. Though not burning yet, it could easily blow and make this already unpredictable job even worse.

The horse, prey animal it was, shied away from the fire. Miranda dismounted and sent her influence to the sparks at the barn. With ease, she took care of the small thing, but as soon as that fire went out, another flicker jumped to the ground near Nan's old car, which was barely recognizable under the snow.

Other snowy piles of vehicles were farther away from the house. How many people were in there? Pops might have more hostages than Riley, and it was still a mystery how he'd gotten the little girl. Not the first time he'd taken a little girl, though, was it?

As if fighting a minor boss in a video game, Miranda pressed her palm to the air and willed the spark underneath the car to die. If it lived and the gas tank ignited, the fire could get out of hand, even for her. She didn't know what the limits of her power were, but in a secret part of her mind, Miranda believed that finding out the true answer would kill her. Not today, though, if she could help it.

She waved Jason closer to her so she could speak into his furry ear. "Can you hear any heartbeats? I don't know where in the house they are."

Lifting his head to listen, his eyes became unfocused. He shook his head in a human side-to-side motion. Then Jason trotted toward the house, everything about his body screaming full alert.

Miranda reached down deep into her fire sense to find the origin point for the blaze. She could switch it off. The fire was mindless and would not win. In a battle of wills, hers was the victor.

At least, that was what she wanted to tell herself. But then her brain lit up with sensory overload.

She grabbed the sides of her head as her mind's eye fought nauseating double vision. Fire in the house. Embers burning near the barn. Tree tops dead for the winter ready to ignite. Paths ready to be blazed in all directions, including one right to her parents' door.

Jason trotted up to her after scouting the perimeter of the house.

[How many?]

He pawed at the ground four times. There might be more than that if the vehicles in the yard were anything to go by.

"Keep listening for heartbeats. Everyone gets out alive."

She stood, fighting the wave of temporary dizziness. Jason came to her side immediately, his shoulder coming up to Miranda's hip. She put her hand at the base of his neck to steady herself. "Take me to the house."

While he led the way, she tried again to connect with her fire sense. It remained an elusive target. Was all her confidence in her abilities a lie when the chips were down? It wasn't like she always got everything right. Jason had to save her from a fire in Ithaca when part of the building collapsed on her.

Miranda didn't have time for self doubt, no matter how much it was making time for her. Flashes of the guilt from burning people alive when she was a little girl riddled her mind. But that was the past. Stay in the moment!

Adding oxygen to fire could make it burn out of control, so they had to be careful how they got in. One of the big dining room windows was broken, so Miranda took a chance at the front door. The door was locked. She used her elbow to break the windowpane in the door and reached through to open it from the inside. The padding of her winter clothing protected her so her arm didn't get sliced by broken glass.

Upon entry, it was clear there were two main areas on fire. The first was in the kitchen, and the second was in the living room fireplace. A greasy trail connected them to each other. Miranda covered her nose and crawled low.

"Hello? Is anyone here?" she shouted.

To Jason, she asked, "They are here, right?"

He bobbed his head once, which probably meant "yes." Using his wolf senses, Jason went hunting for people, and Miranda stood between fires. If she could stop the flames, she could get her family out to safety. As much safety as they could have when there was a snowstorm outside.

Miranda tried again to touch the fire with her mind. She ordered it to end, but the fire mocked her. She had never been good at controlling it when it truly counted. No, that was a lie! She'd mastered her fire control in Ithaca.

As she mentally wrestled it for dominance, she picked up details about the accelerants. The kitchen burn had started with grease, but in the living room there had been paper and... microchips? It had a technological edge.

A forceful tug at the bottom of her jacket brought Miranda out of her meditation. She put her hand on Jason's shoulder, and he guided her to the pantry behind the burning kitchen. The door handle had a chair wedged underneath it so that anyone inside wouldn't be able to get out.

"Hello?" she shouted as she wrestled the chair. It was packed in so tight, Miranda had to kick it to break the legs. "Is anyone in there?"

"We're here!" cried Sheena.

Discarding the broken pieces of the chair, Miranda said, "Move away from the door so I can open it."

"We'll try," Sheena said over a child's wail. "Nan's shoulder might be dislocated, and Sean's ankle is sprained, I think."

"I want my sissy!" shouted Oliver in a plaintive voice that gutted the soul.

Miranda hadn't known that the little boy was there or why. A question for later. She opened the door without thinking to explain that she had a werewolf beside her. The first sounds that rushed out at her were moans of pain and cries of relief. Then the smell of stress and waste followed more obnoxiously than Jessica's peppermint.

Sean was flat on his back, his shoe off and his ankle already swelling. Sheena and Nan were both sitting up, with Nan tenderly holding her left elbow. Oliver was snuggled into Sheena's side, his eyes wide with fear.

"Pops took Riley," Sean whispered.

Crouching in front of them, Miranda asked, "Are there any others?"

Sheena darted a look at Oliver. "No, but I think he might hurt her. He's unhinged and has the history of violence to make it happen."

"Tell me all about it after we get you out," Miranda said.

Nan rasped for breath and turned her gaze on Jason. "You brought a rescue dog with you?"

"Yes, I did," Miranda said. With the house burning around them, maybe they wouldn't get a good enough look at Jason to question where she'd suddenly gotten a giant "dog."

"I love doggies," Oliver sniffed, crawling forward.

"Good! He's going to help get all of you out of the house." Miranda looked at them and formulated a plan. "Sheena, can you help Sean? Oliver, you ride the big dog like he's a pony, okay? I've got you, Nan."

No stranger to trying to ride his Dobermans at home, Oliver easily climbed on to Jason's back. The werewolf led the pack with Sean and Sheena bickering lightly in the middle.

"Just move, Sean! It's like when we did three-legged races as kids."

Miranda ignored them to concentrate on making the path out of the house as fire-free as possible. They had to go through broken furniture and debris that made the once lovely house look like a warzone. After seconds that passed as slowly as the movement of glaciers, the group of six escaped into the night where they could breathe air that was only a little fresher.

Sean and Nan coughed, and Oliver seemed happy to stay on the werewolf's back. The sense of relief at safely getting out was quickly forgotten when the flames licked out windows and across the damaged roof, jumping to the barn. Another lick of flame engulfed Nan's car once again like it was a favorite target.

Miranda pushed back against the destruction pulling her in two directions. She wasn't strong enough to tame it. Nan's car burned quickly as if it were a slip of paper in a campfire. But that was a thing. An object. Not the life of a little girl in the hands of a man who'd already proven he wasn't above hurting people he supposedly loved.

The horse, which had been waiting at the tree line, reached his limit of fear. He fled through the trees, far from the burning menace. Miranda sighed but stood with resolve. Her tasks that night weren't over yet, as much as she, too, might like to run away.

"What are you going to do?" Sheena asked.

"The only thing I can do," Miranda replied. "I'm going in there to save Riley."

CHAPTER TWELVE

"No convenient church or baptistry nearby?" Miranda called out as she charged into the barn with equal parts bravado and anger. "That's what you do with kidnapped little girls, isn't it?"

Her fire sense told her this was where Pops had Riley. Whether or not it was the most prudent idea, she was going on the offensive. Miranda glared at the roof that was now on fire. If she couldn't wrestle control away from the blaze, then she wouldn't have much time to rescue her niece.

Above the urgency of the situation, Miranda couldn't understand why the fires weren't doing what she wanted. Putting out a small fire like this had never been so hard. Surely, it wasn't some mental hurdle because of what she'd been through with Pops. She wasn't willing to give him that much control over her.

"I don't have time to play, Malcolm," she called out. "I'm here for Riley. Give her to me, and we'll go."

"You're a liar!" he shouted as he popped up in the hayloft. "You and Sheena are working against me! I have to take the demon out of this one, too, before it can grow and infect everything."

"You don't get to make those decisions, old man!" Miranda couldn't help shouting, but what else could she do? She wasn't exactly an expert in hostage negotiations. Maybe she'd learn how after she got Riley out of this.

A muffled whine from the loft alerted her to where her niece might be. Carefully, while watching the fire progress overhead, Miranda climbed the side stairs that led up to the hayloft.

As she rounded the landing, Pops threatened her with a pitchfork. "Stay back!"

The situation was not funny in the least, but Miranda laughed. She finally had her pitchfork, sacared villager, and burning torches—AKA the roof—overhead. Now she was truly the monster in Pops's black-and-white movie. But as the saying went, it took one to know one.

For nearly sixty years, Pops had hidden that he'd killed his girlfriend. He'd fled continents because of it, or so it seemed. When Miranda was born with the innate ability to manifest fire, he made his life's mission to break her through her parents. It was twisted, selfish, and so completely wrong that Miranda couldn't understand how he'd made it to eighty years this way.

"Put the pitchfork down, Pops," Miranda said with an affectation of boredom as she stepped into the loft. "I could burn it out of your hand, and then you'd have exactly zero hands that work."

The taunts dried on her tongue when she saw Riley bound to a wooden chair with rope tied around her arms and legs, and her mouth stuffed with a rag to muffle her screams. The chair was precariously perched at the top of a chute, ready to fall to the floor below.

"Riley bug, I'm here to get you. Don't worry," Miranda said softly.

"I told you to get back!" Pops acted seemed ready to charge her with the pitchfork.

Showing her hands empty, Miranda inched closer to him. "Why are you doing this? What could you possibly gain?"

"No, I've already told you enough. You told Sheena, and she came to my Aileen to show her everything she found. She's going to tell everyone!"

"Ah, that's quite reasonable," she said, her eyes still on Riley behind him. "Nan should know she's been married to an arsonist and murderer."

Riley had been the most adept at picking up Sign Language in the last week. Miranda quickly signed a message she fervently hoped the girl would understand. [Watch me. I'm going to burn the rope. Don't be afraid.]

"What are you doing with your hands?" Pops asked, pulling a lighter from his pocket.

Then she took in Riley's wet clothing. It was gasoline, not melted snow. Miranda's intention had been to burn the ropes that surrounded Riley's wrists and ankles, but a stray spark could have dire consequences.

"You're a sick man," Miranda told him. "You picked a little girl because you couldn't grab the one you really wanted to hurt. Is that it?"

She tried to drop again into the mind space that connected her with all the fires around her. The house was unlivable, and Nan's car was close to scrap. Miranda mentally pushed back because the seconds of talking didn't matter. All that mattered was stopping the fire. But when she tried to find her calm and balance, all she saw was Pops's face fourteen years ago, a complete rictus of hate when he tried to drown all life out of her.

Miranda gasped, not for the smoke and flames around them in the barn. Because she still remembered almost drowning. She had hoped learning the secret of her past would free her from its clutches, but it still had insidious influence upon her.

As she fell to the floor, a pair of silver eyes appeared above the landing. Jason, still in his wolf skin, moved silently up the stairs, and Miranda almost laughed to see him. It sounded like a cough as she recovered her wits.

"You have crimes to atone for, Pops. If Sheena doesn't go to the cops with the evidence, I will," she said, standing. "Maybe you got away with a murder in Scotland, but holding Riley hostage? That's not an old crime that haunts you. It's a bad decision you made today."

Miranda leapt toward Pops to take him down to the floor. She never felt so much like a football player, but it gave her angry satisfaction. Then, she concentrated on burning only the ropes that held Riley and not igniting the gasoline. Underneath her, Pops struggled to get her off of him. Miranda held her forearm across his windpipe and obliterated the rope.

"I'm sending you a rescue dog, Riley bug!"

The werewolf leapt into action, kicking the chair out from under Riley while latching onto her clothes with his teeth. The chair tumbled down the chute with the sound of smashing below. Riley slapped the remains of the rope off of her and latched onto Jason. She got on the werewolf's back just as Oliver had done. Jason cautiously walked downstairs with his precious cargo, leaving Miranda alone with her grandfather.

"I want you to know something," she said, leaning heavily into her forearm to subdue him. "You and I are not so different. Two weeks ago, I almost killed a man. I could have done it easily. No one would have known. I have the power and the skill that you will never have."

Miranda backed off him and yanked the man to a standing position. Twisting his arm behind his back, she frog-marched him down the loft stairs. In his ear, she continued her story, though he tried to shake his head to get away from her.

"The man I love doesn't know I almost did that. God help him, he thinks I'm a wonderful person." Miranda almost laughed at that but tightened her hold on Pops. "He is gentle and optimistic. So even though I might be as selfish and destructive as you are, you are *not* the person I'm going to let myself become."

Miranda and Pops walked out of the barn into the open area to witness the wreckage around them. Instead of anger and frustration at the needless destruction, she concentrated on the cleansing power of fire. And of forgiveness. The wound she had to heal was her own.

Keeping hold of Pops with one hand, she put the other hand on her chest and broadcast to all the fire around them. *I am sorry for what I've done, and I forgive myself.*

She and her power were one, and maybe she couldn't focus because of unresolved wounds. But Miranda would start fresh. Instead of telling the fire to stop completely, she called it to her and invited it to live within her. Together, she and the power could combine and become something new for good.

And the fire came, rushing to her over the tops of trees, through the air, and along the ground. Something in it all was happy and hers. Miranda put her arm up to the sky to receive it into herself. It didn't matter that she held the old man to her side; the fire was for her alone.

It consumed her, lighting her hair and skittering along the skin that was still exposed. The power of the fire entered her at every available point, touching her with joy and a sense of satisfaction, a true balm to any homesickness she might have ever felt.

Miranda closed her eyes as the flames built and grew around her. When the brightness outside her eyelids finally decreased, she opened her eyes up to a clear and dark winter night. *Peace.* All was well.

She turned her gaze to the man beside her, and he looked… utterly spooked. He was not burned, but everything else was debatable.

"What are you?" Pops asked.

"The same I've always been. An energy shifter." She was so full of energy, her skin sparkled. It was amusing but would likely fade. "Take a seat. Now we wait for emergency vehicles."

Mere seconds later, Sean's GTO rounded the corner of the burned-out house to the open area where Miranda stood. She put her hand to shield her eyes and was surprised to find that Nan was driving. Her left shoulder was in a makeshift sling thanks to a belt, likely from Sean, but her shifting arm was working just fine.

"The cavalry, Nan?" Miranda said, looking into the car to see Riley and Oliver flanking Sheena in the back seat.

"I told you, lass. You don't sass a Scottish woman."

Miranda smiled for the first time in hours. "No, you don't."

"Your rescue dog brought us Riley and then ran off into the woods," Nan added.

Miranda nodded and fixed her gaze on Riley, who deserved the biggest, tightest auntie hug possible. "Riley bug, you were so brave."

"The bravest," Sheena said with a side hug.

Riley started crying, the kind of pain Miranda knew well. She opened her arms to the little girl, who climbed through the window to get to her. They held on tight until Riley cried herself out.

Jason jogged up a shiny silver thermal suit over the sweats he'd packed in the conveniently hidden drawstring bag. Given his high body temperature, it would keep Jason warm for a while.

"Did I miss everything?" he asked everyone in the car.

"Sissy and I rode the rescue dog," Oliver shouted at him. "He was huge! I want to ride him again."

"That's not up to me," Miranda said. Shifting her attention back to the adults, she asked, "Why were Riley and Oliver even here?"

"Monty and Jessica wanted a date night," Nan told her. "Something about ovulating and not wanting to wait."

So a sex date then. Jason's comment about Jessica's cycle must have struck a nerve.

"I need to tell you something," Miranda told Jason softly as she patted Riley's back.

"With or without an audience?" He inclined his head to the little girl and the family members in the car.

"Small audience," she said. "Let's take a short walk."

Oliver shouted, "I want to go!"

"Come on then," Jason said, extracting the boy out the window.

Neither child had the right kind of clothing to be out in the night, so Miranda walked close beside Jason and created a bubble of warmth to surround all of them. It was so much easier now that she wasn't fighting herself.

Miranda looked up at Jason, his blond hair reflecting the winter light like diamonds. He smiled back at her like she'd created the heavens herself. Though she hadn't, she never wanted to lose the way he always saw the best in her. He had changed her life so much since they first met in August, and mostly it had been good.

"Sure is a lot of talking you're not doing," Jason commented as they paced the road.

"Sorry. Gathering my thoughts. Sometimes small ears have big mouths, and I want only you to know this."

After a few more paces, both children had fallen asleep. Miranda wasted no time in telling Jason the biggest secret she'd withheld from him since they'd been a couple.

"I almost killed John Coleman two weeks ago. I saw him when Lisa and I went out for our girls' night. I was so angry about everything he'd done to us. I'm still angry about it, but it's just another thing that needs to get in line with everything else."

Miranda sniffled Riley's hair, which still had the gasoline smell attached to it. When she was ready, she lifted her head again.

"I can't be the one to decide who lives and dies like an executioner or an assassin. That's what Pops did to Clara and Iain, and I refuse to be like him. I'm still trying to figure out who I am on my own terms, but it won't be like that."

Jason patted Oliver's back and rubbed his cheek on the boy's hair. To Miranda, he said, "We have a lot of pain and a lot of scars."

"We do." She could cosign that as big as John Hancock.

"Was there anything else?"

"Probably. There's always something else. I'll tell you when it comes."

"Deal." He leaned over, kissing her temple. "You did it, Miranda. You saved everyone. I'm so proud of you."

CHAPTER THIRTEEN

On New Year's Eve, Miranda was trying to take an afternoon nap, and sleep would have found her if Riley hadn't found her first. The little girl giggled and thrust a bottle at her that had "Drink Me" written on a sticky note in Jason's handwriting. When Miranda took it, Riley wormed her way under the covers.

"I'm surprised you didn't braid my hair when I was sleeping," she told her niece with a kiss to her head.

"You told me I had to ask," Riley said into Miranda's shoulder.

"That's right, Riley bug. Consent is always important. No one should touch you without your permission."

She opened the bottle and downed its contents as quickly as possible. Tossing it into the waste basket across the room, Miranda softly said, "Three points."

Jason had been mother-henning her with electrolyte drinks in the near week since they'd saved her family from the fire. He meant well, but sometimes his good intentions threatened to make her bladder explode. She had suffered profound exhaustion after the fire. Mostly it was the mental strain of so many intense days in a row, but Jason was helping in the way he knew. Sometimes a person didn't know how to help another, even if they really wanted to try.

Case in point, Riley was quiet and processing what had happened to her. It was a lot for a seven-year-old. Miranda wanted her to know that her best auntie, that being Miranda herself, would never hurt her and would always keep her safe. This was a promise forged in fire.

Miranda hugged the little girl and whispered in her ear. "I should probably get up, huh?"

"Stay here and build a blanket fort," Riley said.

"That is a good idea," Miranda said. "Grown-ups don't get to make enough blanket forts."

Despite the appealing idea, she got up and ran a brush through her hair. Nope, no secret braids while she was sleeping. Then, she splayed her fingers open, and Riley slipped her smaller hand in hers.

Judging from the sounds of the house, Mitch and his family had arrived. The plan was to do fireworks that night, a tradition from warmer climates, and Miranda was going to monitor it all to make sure it didn't get out of hand. Other family members would be coming, though they would not be told about Miranda or Jason's unique gifts.

When she and Riley got to the ground floor, Jackson and his twin sisters, all in their winter gear, were chattering excitedly about going sledding. Riley gave Miranda a look as if to ask for permission to play with her cousins.

"Go! Have fun."

Miranda decided to check the horses in the barn. When they'd returned from their fire adventure, they'd found the runaway horse had safely returned home. She was watching and caring for the animal to make sure he hadn't suffered from any secret injuries.

She slipped on her outerwear, dodging children and conversations like a pro. But Jessica stopped her at the door, her face both serious and sad.

"Thank you again for saving my children."

Jessica had been so thankful in the last week that it was bordering on annoying. Miranda almost missed the tactless, bitchy Jessica. Almost.

"Of course! I love them, you know." She paused and waited for Jessica to look at her. "If you want to show me your appreciation, you can stop calling me Randy. I don't like it. Never have."

"Oh, okay," Jessica said, dabbing at her eyes. "I always thought it was cute. That's all."

With a shrug, Miranda said, "It's what I want."

Leaving that conversation, intent on the barn, Miranda let out a sigh of contentment when she was finally alone with the horses. Sure, she was a fire shifter, but Miranda was also a farrier and horse woman. She had multiple identities that couldn't be conveniently contained.

The next important one on the list was daughter as Michael joined her. He stood beside her but didn't look her in the eyes. It took so long for him to speak that the silence started to get on her nerves.

"What do you need, Dad?"

"A little bit of *auld lang syne* before the New Year, I think. Burns was Scottish."

"I know."

"I'm sorry, Miranda," he blurted.

There were so many things he could and should be sorry for that she had to ask, "Care to be specific?"

He looked at her from his peripheral vision, perhaps irritated that Miranda wanted it said out loud. "For hurting you all these years. For not standing up for you against my father."

"Thank you." Her father's apology was a long time coming. "I don't know what kind of stranglehold Pops had on you, but if you stood up for me from the start, it might have saved us all a world of trouble."

"I don't know how to make this right," he admitted. "Time machines aren't an option."

With a rueful laugh, Miranda said, "I don't, either. Maybe there's a family discount on therapy."

"I had a lot on my shoulders being the oldest son of immigrants," Michael said after several seconds of silence. "It doesn't excuse my behavior, but it explains how I wanted to fit in and be a perfectly unremarkable American. And a fantastic Scot. Because you must be excellent at all things at all times. But you made fitting in impossible."

There was a lot to unpack. She wasn't sure she'd grasped it all, but she still had thoughts left to share.

"My whole life I've felt like a stranger in my own family." Miranda tried her best not to sound accusatory. Or cry. She definitely didn't want to do that. "I've felt so completely alone, and all I wanted was to find someone else like me. We all want to be special, but when we are, it's not always that great."

Michael bit his cuticles and blushed as he darted a glance her way. "Is that why you slept around so much? Because you were lonely?"

Miranda let out a squawk of protest that startled the horses. "You did not just say that!"

"That's the cliche, though, isn't it? Girls who don't feel close to their fathers get attention from somewhere else."

"I'm not playing pop psychologist with that!" Her entire body felt like the prelude to throwing up. "Between you and my murderous grandfather, no wonder I'm messed up!"

Michael let out a heavy sigh. "Oh, yes. That wonderful Lennox legacy."

The family patriarch was in police custody as the main suspect in a cold case in Scotland. He'd thrown Sheena's laptop in the fireplace, not knowing her cousin had her digital murder board backed up and ready to share with authorities. Nan had refused to pay bail for her husband, and none of her sons contravened her wishes.

Miranda shared one last thing with her father. "I'm going to go through my room before Jason and I head back to New York. Maybe I'm no longer sentimental, but most of it is going in the trash. I'll come back from time to time to visit, but not right away."

Michael opened his mouth to speak but immediately closed it and nodded. On a whim, Miranda reached over and took her father's hand in hers. He startled at the touch, which might have been a habit made over the years, but he calmed after a few seconds.

Outside, two vehicles came up the driveway. One was Sheena's SUV, and the other one was Uncle Ronald and Aunt Nancy's car. Miranda and her dad, done with bonding for the moment, went outside to meet them. After parking, Ronald helped his mother out of the car. Nan had a sling on her arm. Considering the woman was eighty-two, she hadn't been hurt as badly as she could have been. Matching his grandmother's injury parade, Sean got out of the passenger side of Sheena's SUV wearing an ankle brace.

"Are you settling in okay, Mom?" Michael asked, leaving a peck on his mother's cheek.

"Anything is better than a burned-out house. I'll be okay," she said. "I've got things to think about while I'm away from your father."

Miranda had wondered if Nan would stay with her parents, but Uncle Ronald and Aunt Nancy had a single-story house. Nan probably felt more comfortable there.

"Caroline has brought over a few real estate listings to get Mom in a new home," Ronald told his brother.

"Some of them are very nice for a single person," she said tartly.

To the side of the conversation, Sean unwrapped a long stick of bubblegum and stuffed it in his mouth. He added another one immediately after that.

"What's this?" Miranda asked, laughing at his gum.

"I think it's safe to say it was time for me to give up smoking. Come over here." Sean opened his arms to give her a hug, and Miranda ran the distance to his embrace. "Are you ever going to tell me how you got that massive rescue dog?"

"You know me. Always did like wild animals more than most people." Patting her cousin's arm, she added, "Some people are exceptions."

Sean nodded. In the days since the fire, he had continued giving Jason driving lessons. The male bonding had been cute, and Jason wasn't grinding the gears so much.

"Speaking of people you actually like, where is that man of yours?"

"Uh..." Miranda looked around. She thought Jason was sledding with the kids, none of whom were in sight. "He's probably around here somewhere. If you want his attention, maybe you need to say something like, 'Vivaldi sucks!'"

"I heard that!" bellowed the man in question. Jason came around the corner in winter gear with Abby, Molly, and Jackson hanging on him like barnacles. "We want hot chocolate!"

Michael led them into the house for their mission of refreshment, but Miranda didn't follow. Sheena tugged on her coat to stay behind. She turned to her cousin, looking into a very sad face.

Sheena sniffed and pulled a tissue out of her pocket. "I keep thinking the fire wouldn't have happened if I hadn't gotten obsessed and showed Nan everything I found."

"Sheen, no!" Miranda hugged her and patted her arm comfortingly when they separated. "It doesn't work like that. If it wasn't you, then something else would have set Pops off. Everything else is an excuse for him not to take responsibility for his own actions."

She sniffed and nodded. "You're right, but I still feel bad."

"You quit that right now," Miranda teased with a playful swat. "I've had enough unearned guilt to cover both of us and a few of the other cousins for a lifetime. Now how about that hot chocolate?"

"That would be great." Sheena strode forward, stopping only when Miranda didn't immediately follow.

"Go on. Call from New York," Miranda told her cousin, waving the phone that had just started buzzing.

Sheena went into the house, and Miranda accepted the call. "To what do I owe the pleasure?"

"Don't have long to talk, sugar. We have New Year's Eve parties to get ready for, but I have some good news I couldn't wait to share with you," Lurlene drawled.

"I could use some of that," Miranda muttered, crossing her arm across her chest in a soothing stance.

"I found a job you can interview for when you get back. They want to meet you to make sure it's a good fit, but it's a done deal if you want it."

"Really?" She couldn't help the squeal that leaked into her voice.

"Yes! A farrier in the Finger Lakes has been looking for an apprentice. There are a number of clients to keep you busy, and there's even a studio apartment with cheap rent. I think you'll like it. I'll send you the information later if you want it."

Miranda would have hugged the woman through the phone if that were possible. "I absolutely want that. Thank you, Lurlene!"

"My pleasure, sugar. Talk to you soon!"

Joy erupted from Miranda. She giggled and twirled in the snow. Muffled applause let her know Jason had come back outside.

"Nice form. Ten out of ten."

"Lurlene got me a job interview!" she said, the smile feeling almost too great to contain.

"Oh, congratulations," Jason said, striding forward to meet her. "That's a great way to start the new year!"

She met him halfway, and once he was in range, Miranda stood on her toes to give him a kiss. As always, they still had much to learn about each other, but with Jason on her side, life was so much better.

After she was done thoroughly kissing him, Miranda rested her forearms on his hips and smiled up at him. "I still need to teach you how to ride while we're here. I might be working all the time when we go back to New York."

"Me riding? That sounds like the start of a joke," he said. "A werewolf rides a horse into a bar..."

Miranda snorted at his joke. "How very western of you."

Taking his hand, Miranda intertwined their gloved fingers. She smiled softly in pleasure. He was with her, and things with Jason were the start of a happier life for her.

"If I don't teach you how to ride horses, maybe you can teach me how to do that thing you want me to do." She let her voice trail off.

It took a few seconds for Jason's face to register that she was talking about pegging. He hadn't been pushy about it, but he'd been obviously sincere in requesting it.

"Oooh, yes, please!" He acted giddy as Jackson or Oliver getting a favorite toy. "Maybe Sean will let you borrow his car again so we can go get some supplies."

"He might. I'll have to ask him. But we should probably go socialize with everyone first," she said, hugging him with one arm and directing him toward the house. "Maybe you can show Nan your thumbs and play something for her."

"That's a good idea, too!"

"Then get on it, soldier," she said, playfully swatting his ass.

Jason jogged ahead, inspired by his musical mission. Miranda followed, admiring the view.

Against all expectations of her visit with her family, she found inner peace and unexpected lightness in her heart. Soon, she'd have a new adventure, whether intimately with Jason or professionally through her new job or something completely unknown. Things were looking up.

EPILOGUE

The only thing Eric Logan could say for certain was that he didn't have a clue about what he was doing. He hadn't even known he had a daughter until a few weeks ago, a Christmas surprise if ever there was one. Her conception had been when he'd been on a drunken bender the week between Christmas and New Year's two years ago to distract himself from the truth of his grandfather's health problems with the most efficient tools possible. Sex and alcohol.

It was now the second week of January, and he was on his way to Kelowna with a big surprise. He and Vanessa had used contraception, but it hadn't worked. Eric was without a doubt the father of Eleanora Frances Baird. She was just like him.

Eric had never met another person like himself before his daughter, but here was a little person he'd helped make with a talent like his own. He never talked about his hidden gift with anyone except his grandfather because Anthony Harris already knew. It appeared, though, that Eric got loose-lipped when he was drunk because he had told Vanessa. That was how she knew to contact him when Ellie started showing her unique power. Had Ellie been a mundane sixteen-month-old, he might have never discovered he had a daughter.

Ellie's diaper needed to be changed, and Vanessa had left him to his own devices with a comment about him having to make up for lost time. So that was how he found himself in the men's room at SeaTac, waiting for a connecting flight back to British Columbia so he could introduce her and his baby mama to his grandfather.

Weren't sixteen-month-olds usually potty trained by now? He felt embarrassed for himself and for his daughter. He put his hands on the changing table and sighed like it was the end of the world.

He thought he'd been alone in the bathroom, but a tall, blond man stepped out of a stall. The stranger went to the wash basin, and Eric regarded him. If he hadn't been all thumbs with this new fatherhood situation, he might have looked closer. Most of Eric's relationships had been with women, but plenty of men had caught his eye over his twenty-four years.

The other man, who had startling silver eyes, stared at him intently, his mouth slightly open with lips that needed to be kissed. Eric mentally kicked himself for even thinking that. He dipped his head and went back to his daughter, who was wiggling restlessly on the changing table and chattering about something. He hadn't known her long enough to interpret her sounds.

"Do you need help?" the man asked, his voice a surprise in the room. As he spoke, he held one hand in a fist with the thumb sticking up and moved the fist forward on the flat of his opposite hand. Was that Sign Language?

Frowning in confusion, Eric admitted, "I need to change my daughter's diaper, and I've never done it before."

"I got a little experience doing that with my girlfriend's nephew," he said, stepping closer to Eric and Ellie.

Girlfriend. Right. So probably not someone who'd step back into the stall for a blowie. Not a thought he should be having in front of his daughter while her mother waited at their gate.

Despite feeling the body heat of the stranger beside him, Eric faced his fears and removed the diaper, wiped his daughter clean, front and back. It was a little disgusting as he soiled his hand in the process. Not the suave impression he wanted to make in front of a hot guy, even one with a girlfriend.

Then he put a fresh diaper on Ellie and assessed his work.

"Good?" he asked her.

"Dah!"

It might have meant "down." If he didn't do something quickly, Ellie would likely jump off the changing table. Eric helped her down and then washed his hands, taking care with lots of soap.

When he was done, he turned back, and the man was still there. He'd raised his hand, hovering near Eric's cheek, and was looking at him in fascination. Maybe this was a pickup in the men's room after all. Not one he could pursue despite the intriguing vibe the blond man gave off. Eric swallowed hard.

"You're an energy shifter," the stranger said. "So is your daughter. Not the same power as you and not fire..."

Oh, he had a power all right, and Ellie's was different from his.

"You're so beautiful."

The tone the other man used was hushed and reverent.

It wasn't the first time Eric had been called beautiful. He stood on the short side of average at five-foot-eight, and his muscular body was compact from dance and aerial arts. His midnight black hair and bright blue eyes completed the package that was often called beautiful instead of rugged and hypermasculine.

Eric's mind caught up with the words beyond the compliment. "Fire?"

"My girlfriend," he dropped his voice to an intimate whisper, "she controls fire. Her aura looks like a living fire. But yours doesn't. You look... blue. I don't think you control water. You don't *smell* like water."

The man leaned forward to sniff him, and Eric put up his forearm to shove back. "Get off me!"

Ellie must have picked up on Eric's distress. She sent out a tremor for their own private earthquake. "No!"

The man shifted his attention to Ellie and bent down low to greet her. From his kneeling position, he declared, "Her aura is brown like the earth. Clear like whiskey, though. I guess that leaves air and water out there somewhere. Miranda will be happy to learn she's not alone."

He stood and faced Eric. "I probably seem like a creep to you. I'm sorry. You don't know me, and this is a weird place to talk about secret important things. But... one last question. Have you ever met any other energy shifters?"

No. Eric had thought he was a dangerous anomaly until he met Ellie. Given that Eric could manipulate electricity, sometimes to fatal results, he thought that was a one-off event.

"Only the two of us," he finally allowed.

He'd been on the defensive the whole time, but Eric decided to ask about the auras. "You can *see* the color of my power? Like I'm an anime character?"

"I can," he answered, crossing his arms over his chest. "You're as bright as the full moon."

The phrasing tickled Eric's brain. He laughed unexpectedly and gathered Ellie and her things. "I suppose that makes you a werewolf then."

He was still laughing to himself when the other man said, "Yes, I am. There are many others like me, but they know nothing of energy shifters like you."

"Energy. Shifter." Eric latched onto the term.

"If I'm a shape shifter, and I am, then you and your daughter shift energy. It makes perfect sense."

"Sure it does. But you think you're a werewolf. And I think that's loco."

Eric was done with this conversation in this location. He had to get out and go back to Vanessa so they could take their flight.

He picked up Ellie and stomped out of the bathroom. Then he looked around to orient himself to find his gate. Behind him, he could feel the deranged man who thought he was a werewolf. Eric also heard the warm voice of a woman calling out.

"Jason, what took you so long?"

He wasn't, nor had he ever been, a man named Jason, not even in his darkest inclinations. But the prickle at the back of Eric's neck made him turn toward the voice.

It belonged to a petite, redheaded woman, her long hair in a French braid. She wore jeans and a flannel shirt over a t-shirt. The red hair was attention-getting because it looked like it was real instead of a gift from a bottle. While he was studying her, he realized that this must have been the fire-powered girlfriend of the werewolf.

She also held a violin case, which amused Eric more than it should have. His high school girlfriend played violin, often topless when he was around. He'd developed a *thing* for naked violinists. Not that it usually came up in first conversations.

"Do you play violin?" he asked the redhead.

"No, but he does," she answered, passing the case to the man whose name seemed to be Jason.

Eric glanced at the blond to his right. No, imagining him naked playing violin wouldn't be too much of a hardship.

Jason used rapid Sign Language to tell his girlfriend something. She approached, putting her hands out to make him stop signing.

"What's going on?" she asked, an unsure smile sliding over the three of them as they stood together.

"He's an energy shifter, Miranda."

The emotions that played over her face changed quickly, but Eric recognized all of them. Fear and disbelief chased by hope. So much hope.

Setting Ellie down, he stepped the last few inches closer to her and politely held out his hand. "Hi. I'm Eric."

"Miranda." Her voice was a whisper that he wasn't sure he'd actually heard. As slow as a glacier, she put her hand in his.

Once they were skin to skin, Eric felt her power communicate with his own the way he felt Ellie's earth power when they touched. The child's energy behaved differently than his own, and Miranda's energy was different still. It was wild and full. When touching her, he could smell sulfur and memories of blazes gone by. It was like the fire version of petrichor. There had to be a word for that.

And Eric could feel Miranda's fire setting off every one of his synapses. Cautiously, he pushed back with his own energy, and she gasped. Instead of demanding he stop, Miranda came closer into his space. Tears sprang to her eyes as she stood, her arms wrapped much more intimately around him than the usual for strangers in an airport.

"Are there more like us?"

It was a prayer, a feeling he knew well. He'd been alone until he met Ellie only a few weeks ago.

"My daughter," he whispered, so close to her they could almost be sharing the same skin.

Beside them, Jason held Ellie in his arms. Eric could have kicked himself for temporarily taking his mind off her, but the little girl didn't look bothered in the least. She tugged at Jason's copious hair and happily babbled about something.

Miranda put her hand to her mouth, and the tears started to fall harder. Without much thought about propriety, Eric wrapped his arms around her. It seemed the most natural thing in the world to do. Then he felt her energy reaching out to him, communing with him beyond words. Ellie must have understood on an instinctual level, because she reached her pudgy hands out to touch both of them. They stood entwined with the supposed werewolf standing watch over them.

When at last he let Miranda go, Eric took Ellie back. Jason slipped his free arm around Miranda's waist, and she matched him with an arm around his. With the palm of her other hand, Miranda touched Eric's chest, a tentative smile on her face.

He took a deep breath, because looking at both of them together was like facing the embodiment of bisexual panic. Or maybe that was pansexual panic. What did one call it when a werewolf was involved in the equation?

"Are you really a werewolf?"

Jason smiled at him without showing teeth. "I am."

He ruffled the hair off the back of his neck and bent closer to show Eric a double helix tattoo at the top of his spine.

"It goes all the way down," Miranda added with an impish tone.

Eric blinked. "How is that proof you're a werewolf?"

"It's one of the marks from the genetics lab in Evanston, Illinois."

As Jason talked, the color of his irises changed from silver to red. It was peculiar, but when he smiled and squeezed the woman at his side, Eric had to know what was happening.

"I'm touching him with my fire. He's like a vessel I can fill with my energy without hurting him." Adding a quiet whisper, she said, "I don't know if it's because he's a werewolf or because I love him. But no pain."

Eric's mother had loved his little sparks. Both his parents, being academics, found their son's electrical mutation fascinating. Too bad it was the thing that killed them.

Despite his old scars, Eric's hand clenched. He wanted to touch Jason for a handful of reasons that he didn't want to get into. But the other man made it easy to give in to temptation.

"You can touch me." Jason gently took Eric's hand and placed it directly on his spine by his hip. "Be gentle."

He took a deep breath while keeping eye contact. Then Eric let his electricity rise and race along synapses in all directions. It was so odd to let his barrier down because Eric had not shared his secret with others, not even previous lovers. Who were these strangers to know anything about him?

But then Eric saw Jason's silver eyes change to blue. When they did, he shifted his weight and reached out to Eric.

"Jason?" Miranda asked at his panting breath.

"I'm fine. I'm fine... but Eric needs to pull back or I'm going to come all over myself in the middle of this airport."

"I'm sorry!"

He apologized for propriety, not that he truly felt it. An orgasm was simply synapses firing in a certain way. There was electrical logic to it. Experiments in orgasms would be lovely to try with willing subjects.

"She lights me up like a candle when she orgasms, so I guess it's to be expected."

Miranda shook her head at her boyfriend and then put her free hand on Eric's cheek. He memorized her soft face with brown eyes and a pert nose. The sweet moment was augmented by Ellie who grabbed at Jason, too. Eric disentangled her before Jason's eyes could turn brown or green or whatever color went with Ellie's earth energy.

"Where did you grow up?" Eric asked.

"Montana. You?"

"British Columbia. I moved to Kelowna when I was six, after my parents—"

He was willing to talk to her and learn all about her, but he was saved exchanging his tale of woe by the phone ringing in his pocket. Vanessa was telling him to get his ass in gear. The intercom announced the last boarding call for his flight, so her warning was no joke. He hadn't realized that he'd spent so much time with the couple and let out a sigh of deep sadness.

"That's me. I have to go. Now."

With a sense of regret for something ending before it could truly begin, Eric fixed their images in his mind. Then he picked up Ellie and ran across the airport to meet Vanessa and eventually their families in Kelowna.

Somewhere behind him, in a world he couldn't know, was a woman who controlled fire and a werewolf, one of many. He didn't know how to find Miranda or Jason, but he had their names and the location of the lab where the werewolf was created. It was a start.

AUTHOR NOTES

I've always been one of those people who stayed for the credits of a movie or read all the liner notes on an album. That extends to acknowledgments like this in other people's books. I have a lot of people to thank because making a book publication-worthy, even as an indie writer, requires the help and support of a lot of people.

Here are some of the essential people who helped me bring this story to you.

Brainstormers: Annie, Hope, and Meri

Beta Readers: Amur, Annie, Erica, Hope, Meike, Meri, and Monna

Blurb Polishers: Annie, Jill, Monique, and Shelby

Cover Crew: Annie, Cathy, Hope, and Meghan

Thanks to Ashley and Jen for reminding me that self-care is important and burn-out is no joke.

Additional thanks to my editor Ashley for doing what she does so well. She can always find ways to improve my writing while still making it all sound like my voice. As a writer, that was something that was extremely important to me.

***

AFTER MEETING ERIC and Ellie in the epilogue, you might be curious how many different kinds of energy shifters there are. The characters themselves don't know yet, but the answer is five: Fire, Earth, Air, Water, and Electricity.

We will see more energy shifters as I continue to grow the series. Some will know Jason and Miranda directly; others won't. I am unlikely to ever write a character for this series who can master all five energies.

Werewolves won't always be a secret group of people and will "come out of the kennel" a few years after this story is set. Energy shifters may be able to hide in plain sight a while longer due to the fact that it's not easy to recognize each other without being in close proximity.

There will be more for this series,. Stay tuned, and thank you for reading!

-JDC

CREDITS

Cover by VILADESIGN, purchased through SelfPubBookCovers.com

Cover titling by JD Cadmon

Editing by Ashley Rayner, senior editor at Inkwell's Editorial Services

Did you love *A Fire In Her Bones*? Then you should read *Let's Bake A Deal*[1] by JD Cadmon!

JD CADMON [2]

When sex-shop owner Eva Stephens meets ambitious baker Remo Belli over the trash one morning, they quickly whip up a half-baked scheme to benefit both of their businesses.

Remo, home again after completing his pastry arts degree, wants to take over the family bakery, but his nonna won't hear of it unless he's in a relationship that might lead to grandchildren. Asexual Remo finds that outcome highly unlikely, but fake-dating Eva for six months might be the secret ingredient to changing his nonna's mind.

---

1. https://books2read.com/u/bPgDL7

2. https://books2read.com/u/bPgDL7

In exchange, Remo will help Eva entice hesitant community members through the doors of The Love Shack by creating tempting treats for the sex-positive shop's educational programs. Eva, who has been struggling to keep her shop afloat, is more than willing to test his recipe for success.

It's strictly business—no feelings have to be involved. Too bad falling for each other is as easy as pie.

<u>Content Warning</u>: Mild depictions of aphobia and homophobia

Read more at https://jdcadmon.carrd.co/.

Also by JD Cadmon

A Feral Spark
A Feral Spark
A Fire In Her Bones

Belli & the Beat
Let's Bake A Deal

Watch for more at https://jdcadmon.carrd.co/.

About the Author

JD Cadmon is the pen name for a Louisiana-based writer who loves scifi, fantasy, and a good romance. Preferably with dashes of comedy and adventure. You know you've got something from JD Cadmon when there are bisexual main or secondary characters living their best lives and the text is full of puns, banter, and general wordplay.

JD has a bachelor's degree in music education with an applied specialty in percussion and a master's degree in library science. She sings and plays multiple instruments beyond percussion. She also is an avid language learner, having seriously studied six of them, and she dreams of becoming competent in American Sign Language.

The love of music and language is so strong that it can't help but be reflected in her characters.

JD also loves photography, astronomy, traveling, and returning home when the adventure is over. Bucket list destinations include Iceland and New Zealand beyond a quick plane change in the Auckland airport.

Read more at https://jdcadmon.carrd.co/.

www.ingramcontent.com/pod-product-compliance
Lightning Source LLC
Chambersburg PA
CBHW071326140726
47996CB00005B/1832